COLOR

— a novel —

Sandi Russell

First published 2013 by Mosaic Publishing

ISBN 978-0-9567816-7-3

Library of Congress Cataloging-in-Publication Data
1. African Americans — Fiction. 2. Native Americans — Fiction.
3. New York, N.Y. — Fiction. 4. Virginia — Fiction.
I. Title

BIC classification
1. FA — fiction, modern and contemporary (post c.1945)
2. HBJ — humanities, history, regional and national 1KB (North
America)

Typeset in Myriad by Mosaic Print & Design, Middleton-in-Teesdale.
Printed and bound in Great Britain.

Mosaic (Teesdale) Ltd,
Moor Edge, Snaisgill
Middleton-in-Teesdale
County Durham
DL12 0RP UK

www.mosaicteesdale.co.uk

For all my people
here and gone
known and unknown

When you yet knew you still knew nothing.
The River sang and sings on.

Maya Angelou, 'On the Pulse of Morning'.
Inaugural poem for President Clinton,
January, 1993

I am the American heartbreak –
Rock on which Freedom
Stumps its toe –
The great mistake
That Jamestown
Made long ago.

Langston Hughes, 'American Heartbreak',
The Panther and the Lash (1967)

CONTENTS

THREE

TIDEWATER COUNTY, VIRGINIA

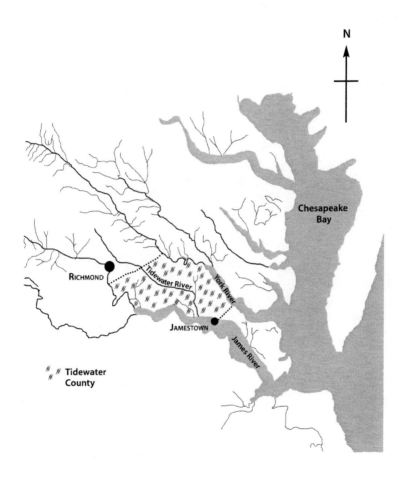

The main action of this story takes place
in Manhattan and Virginia,
between 1980 and 1998.

FAMILY TREE

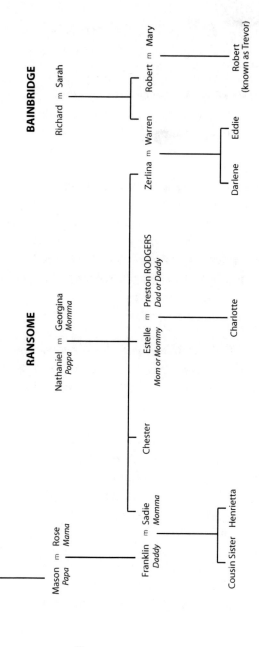

THE RIVER SPEAKS

Flowing I am ancient I am young.
Full of fresh water touched with salt,
I am flowing to the James independent
kissing shores and offering blessings.

I am flowing southeast, bearing chants and songs
for me, loved and cherished.
Placidly I glide as I have for year upon year of sunrise.
I have dancers in my waters, divers, contemplators;
crabs that caress my sloping shores,
oysters, mussels, multi-colored fish
all frolic in my narrow stream.
I am flowing.

Full of wealth and wondrous knowledge, I am a silent giver.
Shore-dwellers take from me with spear and net and hand,
sing praises to my saltwater, my freshwater, my mud.
I am flowing.

With steady path and watchful eye
I see my neighbor change dress for me.
Bursts of colored brightness,
greens variant of leaf and hue and brown stark stillness
all speak their say, sing their story.
I am flowing.

Bronze worshiping people have made paths
for bounty, for sustenance, for beauty.
Gatherers of spirit and sap, they bow

to growth, to reap, to mystery.
Shaded by hickory, black walnut and various cousins,
hands hold mulberries, plums, persimmons
grapes and strawberries.
And the yellow stalk that is life to all,
grows golden in blue skies and kisses the gods.
I am flowing.

Bear and bobcat, turkey and their kin
know well my adjoining green tapis,
while in my marshes racoon, opossum, beaver and muskrat
marry land to water.
I am flowing.

A milk-white madness colors
my waters red.
I am flowing sickness, I am flowing deceit,
I am flowing lost.
Time's new hand, progress, has touched me,
making me spill my treasures and slow my pace.

But I shall see you New World
I shall mark your mistrust and
mock your masterliness.

For my eye is ever-clear
my path unchanging and my story there
for all who hear me:
I am flowing, I am flowing, I am flowing.

ONE

PALETTE

I WAS sitting with my crayons, outside on the porch, when my little cousin Eddie came by Aunt Sadie's, smelling like peanuts. His red and blue striped tee-shirt hung loose, except where the heat grabbed it, his tan shorts torn and grass-stained, bare brown feet ringed in dust.

'Is it always hot like this down here in Virginia?' I said. 'Do you have a wintertime?'

'Yeah, we got Christmas, if that's what you mean.'

'No, I mean, real cold and lots of snow, like in New York, where I live.'

'Every once in a while, but most times it just be cool, not cold. I wanna come to New York. I seen them red fire engines and I heard about that place called the Apollo on 125th Street. It real famous and everybody that play there be real famous too –Smokey and the Miracles, James Brown, Jackie Wilson – all them people. You been there?'

'No, I wanted to go, but Daddy said there'd be too many crazy niggers and I might get hurt or something. I sure wanted to, though.'

'Your daddy talk like Trevor's. In fact, Trevor be sayin terrible bad things about colored people, said he learnt it from his daddy and mommy, and they should know. He and Darlene got in a fight. Trevor be fightin his own cousin, and she a girl! She fought him good though, but I could see her eyes wet up when he pulled that long, black hair of hers. She told him he might be pretty, but as far as she was concerned, he was just pretty stupid. She some smart girl, don't you think? And I thinks she's the prettiest girl in all of Tidewater County.'

'Yeah', I said, remembering when the two of us went on a long walk last summer and talked about all kinds of things, especially boys. But Darlene kept going back to some kind of history of the family. I just wanted to sit by the river and look at the trees and feel the breeze, what little there was of one. I tried to listen, but I kept drifting off, playing with my crayons and dying to sit down and draw.

3

'What you got there, Charlotte?' Eddie leaned towards my lap where I had my piece of paper. 'That real good, Charlotte, real good. You gonna be an artist?'

I looked down at what I'd done and saw Daddy's angry, bunched-up face looking at it too.

'No, I don't think so …'

Marsha, an old friend from childhood, had stopped by my studio one promising spring day before the show, with wine and lots of gossip. As I poured, I saw her reacting to my newest canvas. Her forehead was folded like an accordion:

'Girl, what is this? I don't understand it. I think I'm a fairly intelligent woman, but whatever you're doing here just doesn't speak to me. Do other people understand it? Like it?'

'Yeah, quite a few. Even some of those snotty critics seem to know what they're talking about. But I want to reach people like you. You really can't get into it, can you?'

'No, girlfriend, I'm really sorry. What you've been doing lately is just beyond me. I like the colors and all, but what the hell are you supposed to be saying?'

'I'm trying to get to our core, our essence. I don't know, it's hard to express. I'm trying to capture the energy, the originality, the way we've had to improvise all of our lives; make a way out of no way, find music in a cotton field, beauty in a life of bondage, color in a city of grey and life in the grip of death.'

'Girl, I think I understand what you're saying, but why don't you do some stuff like Basquiat? Now, I can get into that. It's a little more explicit, you know what I mean? I liked the work you did before all this abstraction: the stereotypes and everything. That was hard-hitting, girl.'

'I'm looking for a new way to express an old problem. I need to explore a different space.'

'Yeah, well a lot of those critics like what you are doing, so go on ahead. But do you really like it, Charlotte?'

A few months after I saw my friend Marsha, Cheryl Washington of the Studio Museum of Harlem was checking out my latest work. I was so anxious that even though she was smiling and moving her arms about like she was excited, I couldn't hear her. It was like my nerves had closed down my ear-drums and all I could do was stand and grin. And then finally, sound came: 'I really like this new work you're doing. In a few of them, though, I feel something is missing, but that might just be me. Overall, it really has impact. Would you like to have a showing at the Studio, say, in about six months?'

'Only six months?' God, this was incredible.

'Yeah, of course. I'd love to.'

I thought, 'Well, I'm on my way. Heaven only knows where, but I'm on my way.'

Going to hang the show was the hardest part. There they all were, waiting for me. Leaning against the wall, my pictures spoke of many things. Some of them so vibrant with color, it was hard to look. I had tried to make their line and curve come together in an effort to highlight, as Romare Bearden said, 'the innerness of the Negro experience.' I had heard a talk he gave and seen his work. It shook me so — the colors, the shapes, the beautiful truth of it — that I was wrenched from my complacent little place, aching to paint until my arms fell off. The other work I did was clearer in purpose: a dismantling of all those sickening black stereotypes. I just turned them on their heads. Then, the others: angular shapes and echoes of African masks, long limbs and gracefulness, filling canvas after canvas.

That afternoon, just before the opening of the exhibit, nerves made me rigid. Was I any good? Were they going to understand what I was trying to do? Why didn't I just stay at home? God, I hated these openings. I went to the mirror on the far side of the room and stared: an ivory-colored face with freckles and a hint of red; eyes that darted rather than look inside themselves — big black pools of confusion. Did my work express what roiled inside me? I no longer knew. And what about this anger? Where was I going to put all that? It stuck to my insides like adhesive, never emerging; a shock here, a statement there, but no real confrontation. I guessed that part of the reason was I really didn't know why, mostly railing against any old thing. Maybe I just didn't want to know why. But this was no time to confront messy emotional stuff; I had an audience to conquer.

I sucked in the air and pulled myself up. Taller, straighter, I walked towards the heavy door, steadying myself for the hard bite of a Manhattan event.

'Blackness is a state of mind.' The words caught me as I started down the stairs into the gallery's buzz and laughter. With my hands wet against the sides of my dress, I stepped in.

Another voice, thick and resonant, rose as I passed: 'No, it's not. What are you talking about? It's a reality, a state of being. It's not a mind-set, you know.'

The reedier voice responded now: 'You have to admit that blackness in America is a spectrum. A bit of all things, all colors. That's a truth we don't like to look at. At least some of us don't.'

The voices quieted as I moved away from the one motioning, in red, green and black. The other, light, in all black, seemed to be diminishing. The air conditioner was on, but heat still grabbed us by the neck. The clinking glasses sweated and glistened as I tried to smile a smile of the confident.

It was my show — CHARLOTTE RODGERS: NEW COLORS, June 1980. Bits of my mind, my search, steadied themselves against the celery-colored walls. I should be used to this by now, but never was. New York critics, collectors, and poseurs: the whispers, the caustic words, and the supercilious flash of lips when they saw me.

It was a good mix: black, brown, red, yellow and white, in all permutations filling up the space. Faces uninterested, anxious, bored, engaged and fascinated were all there for my exhibit. That's what I liked to think, although I knew that many just wanted to see themselves reflected in others' eyes. Watch themselves mingle among the others watching themselves, all congratulating each other for knowing this was a hip place to be. Did anyone understand the paintings in that room? Why these forms, shapes and colors came together the way they did? Did I?

It was a success. My body felt limp as I kicked over plastic cups, paper plates, programs left on the gallery floor. I flung myself onto a chair and looked. They were accomplished, polished, engaging. But Cheryl and Marsha were right. Something was missing. I saw it then. I knew it in my heart before, but couldn't face that I didn't know what it was. I still didn't. Christ, what was it?

I picked up the newspaper that lay on the floor beside me and browsed through the Arts section. The article leapt out:

>Dwayne Dillon's done it again. A triumph. His acting is going from strength to strength. And his inviting, enigmatic face keeps you frozen in your seat. The camera loves him. He is all-encompassing.

It went on praising him and the film. I could just see his smile.

Wondering how he was, I flipped back to those days in Tidewater County, when he was just Trevor, my distant cousin, and he had enveloped me in all his fineness. Sunny days and sweet talk, but mostly about himself. Did he ever think of home anymore, I wondered? Tidewater County must seem far away from him now, after living the high-life in Hollywood and Connecticut. It seemed far away from me too, even though it was my parents' home now that they'd left New York and gone back.

I bet Trevor was still running away from dirt roads, juke joints, women shouting 'Amen' and passing out in church. Fleeing from poverty and a past he didn't want to look at or understand. He was so beautiful, so unhappy in his skin. He had everything. Was wanted by everyone, everywhere. Yet, he was miserable. Thinking about him began to make me uneasy. I tried to think of different things.

My eyes roamed the room, finally resting. It was a red splash, taking prominence in the painting that caught me. It was the color of a cardinal, the bird that brightened the skies of Tidewater. I could see my little yellow arms turning red-brown under that exploding sun:

Mommy and me and train-whistles and sweat and little pink pinafores. Shoe-boxes of fried chicken, stares and, 'Ain't she the cutest thing?' Sandy soil and hungry eyes and questions, questions, questions. Bare feet and peanuts and Dr Pepper. Pigs and rust and loss. Parched grass, mosquitoes — madness.

I jumped up as it hit me. Tidewater — that was it. Maybe the answer was there, the missing part of me. That old river. That fogged-up history. My people: whites, blacks, Native Americans, all the jumbled pieces. I was going to go and confront it: that family of mine, its truths, its lies.

DRIVING LESSONS

A MONTH or so after the show, the phone rang. Mom's soft, sad voice said, 'You've got to come down now, Charlotte. Franklin's mother, Rose, she died. I know this isn't your favorite place, but I really think you should show.'

'Oh, don't worry, Mom. I was just planning to come anyway.'

'You were? I don't understand.'

'Well, you see, it's kind of complicated. Let's just say I'm missing something.'

'You're missing something? Charlotte, are you taking drugs? You confuse me sometime. You've got everything. Why are you talking about missing something?'

'Mom, I just need to find the answers to some questions.'

'Answers to some questions? You surely aren't going to find any here. Wouldn't it be easier in all those libraries in New York?'

'I'm not looking for those kinds of answers. Let's not get into it now, Mom. I'll explain when I get there.'

I could hear my mother's deep sigh. The child she could never quite fathom: after all these years, the barriers, the opaqueness.

'Alright, darling. We'll talk when you get here.' Her voice was a trail of knowing disappointment.

Family, my family. In New York, I didn't have to explain it, not even to myself — especially to myself. But, driving South in this sleek rented sky-blue Audi convertible, the whole living mess of it came rushing at me, as the miles swept by: a maelstrom of faces, voices and unspoken half-truths. I felt myself being pushed forward, as if on a conveyor belt, with no way out.

What the hell was that woman talking about? 'Blackness is a state of mind?' Christ, if it was, a lot more folks would be well and alive today.

9

She must have been one of these desperate academics, trying to move a reality into some convoluted theory, just so she'd have something to write about. Shit, I know it's real, as many times as I've had to deal with it: all that rancid, deadly, mess that permeates this entire country.

But I do kind of get what she was trying to say. What *does* blackness mean? So many of us an amalgam, never wanting it that way. Now, what should we call ourselves then? African-English-Scottish-Irish-Spanish-Chinese-Native-Americans? (And who knows about Italian, German or Polish? How about Japanese? Or anything else?)

But if we stopped being black, then who would claim the culture? The culture that moulded and made America. The culture that America is known for. All that glorious, vibrant, shouting, resilient culture. All that richness. All that life.

As the spiraling, cold, grey buildings gave way to tedious rectangles that shoved hard against each other, the world of cheap convenience fenced in either side of the highway. After miles of neon signs winking and billboards announcing: 'All You Can Eat – Only $8.00', the garish declarations finally fell away and cool, calm greenness took precedence. You would have thought that the rolling expanse before me would have eased my mind, but my shoulders were still nudging my ears as they had when I left New York.

I had to admit that running into my aunt's husband, Franklin, was not my idea of fun. He'd been so strange for so long, it was hard to know what to make of it. When I was little, he was full of joy and surprises. Then, like lightning, he was a changed man. Used to sit on the steps and stare into the horizon. If you spoke to him, he just nodded or spoke like a voice lost in a wind tunnel. Nothing excited him, nothing stirred him. Yet, he seemed to be waiting for something; every once in a while, his eyes would light up as if he had seen the shiniest, most radiant thing. Then nightfall.

His wife, Sadie, Mom's sister, was just the opposite. In your face. You felt her presence for miles. Big and noisy, she too, had changed. In those bright, easy summers, she used to make me the most precious little dresses, saying: 'Bet you can't get anything look this good and special in them high-class stores y'all buy from.'

As I was about to say, 'Yes I can. I've got lots of pretty dresses Mommy bought me', Mom burst out with: 'Oh no, we could never find anything as pretty as what you do. You put your stamp on it, too. Can't nobody do that.'

Aunt Sadie would beam and be so happy that she'd rush into the kitchen and start slicing up potatoes and heating up oil. Splat, those potatoes would pop into that hot fat and in a few minutes all of her children would be buzzing around her waiting for their potato chips. Everything would be all smiles, until Henrietta, with her bouncing, blond curls, lifted up her face, full of hope, hands outstretched and wanting. A dark cloud then passed over Sadie's face and filled the whole room. All you could see was Sadie's fury and Henrietta's hurt and longing.

As the car cruised along Route 95, the dense green that had fringed the sides of the road began to look weary from heat's hand and turn into tufts of straw-colored grass, some with tips of brown. This new landscape seemed to lessen any sense of delight or expectation. It was then I remembered the dry, prickly grass as I pulled up my little yellow dress and squatted: 'But Mommy, somebody will see me.'

'No, honey, I'm in front of you,' she'd say. 'Go on now.'

It was never easy, never comfortable, always worrying about bugs and dirt and any little creatures that could come along. And snakes. I was always afraid of snakes.

Well, I thought. At least I don't have to do that anymore. And I can stop and eat wherever I want now, although I wouldn't say I saw the friendliest of faces once I crossed the Mason-Dixon line. But at least I could sit down in peace, if not in relaxation.

As I passed the sign showing the exit to Washington DC, I saw the majesty of the Capital Building and its Palladian adjunct, the White House. I was nowhere near either building, but the image of them sat squarely in front of my eyes like a roadblock. Nebulous symbols, these.

Nothing as clear-cut as freedom and democracy came to mind when you looked at them. For my folks, did they ever live up to their promise? There was so much possibility in those two buildings, but now, a new wind was blowing and from where I was sitting, it was so chill that I could have used an overcoat in 90-degree weather.

The irksome image before me faded and soon gave way to the wide and welcoming Chesapeake Bay. So placid, you almost wanted to drive to its edge and jump in. For millions though, it might as well have been quicksand. For the brown, beaten and bewildered, the hands and limbs that made this the most prosperous nation in the world, it signaled living death. I could never rest easy in the South, maybe because the South couldn't yet rest easy with itself.

Inching closer to Richmond, a tightness gathered around my throat and I wanted to spin the car around and head back North. Here I was, in the seat of the Confederacy, with its broad, sylvan avenues and overpowering statues of Lee, Davis and Jackson, waving swords, surrounded by cannons. Further along stood Arthur Ashe, wielding a tennis racket — their idea of equality. Old Glory flapped and waved from just about every porch and the vibrant pink of the crape myrtle underlined everything.

I passed Richmond's largest store, Malmeyer's, and recalled how Cousin Sister, Sadie's daughter, got so excited when my mother took us shopping there. She ran from rack to rack, touching all the garments, even rubbing some against her deep brown cheek, which caused a little problem with the saleslady that Mom soon settled. We had to 'hush' her constantly, especially around the jewelry section. She was overwhelmed and her cries of joy and astonishment echoed throughout the store. I wanted to run away, but Mom just grabbed my hand and said, 'She's just very happy. Try to understand.'

Well, I tried, but most of the time I found myself turning away as if I didn't know her when she shrilled: 'Oh, this is so pretty. Lord, all of it pretty. I wants it all. Can I at least have some, Aunt Estelle, can I?'

She came to New York and stayed with us when she was fourteen. She said she was going to make a whole lot of money and go buy all those things she'd seen in the magazines and on the television. 'Sure,' I said. She replied, 'Y'all see. I'm gonna have all that sparkle and pretty.'

One day, I went with some friends to visit Cousin Sister at Woolworth's food counter, where she had gotten a job. She looked so funny. Perched on top of her long, shiny, jet-black hair was a little angular white paper cap. It kept sliding to the side and front, even though she tried to fasten it with a hair-pin. 'What y'all want?' she said, her voice shaking ever so slightly.

We all ordered hamburgers and cherry cokes. It was too painful to watch. Clumsy and unsure of herself, she dropped things and managed to get our order confused with somebody else's. The hamburgers weren't cooked and she had to do them again. I was busy trying to stop my girlfriends from sniggering or downright laughing, but I was having a hard time keeping a straight face myself.

'Y'all goin shoppin? When y'all goin? Can I come? I be finished at four o'clock.'

Shopping was always on her mind. I wondered if anything had taken its place or was it still consuming her?

I drove out of Richmond and onto the road leading to Tidewater County. After a few miles road names, names of stores and buildings all bore my mother's family moniker — Ransome: Ransome Road, Ransome Avenue, Ransome General Store. This gave me a bit of assurance. An uneasy embrace.

The sign read 'Exit 325 for Bucksloe Beach'. I remembered when Franklin, Sadie, Cousin Sister and her sister, Henrietta, Mom and I all piled into that old Chevy station wagon they had and headed there.

'Why does Henrietta have blond hair?', I wondered, but when I asked Mommy, she just said, 'Shhh,' Franklin cleared his throat and Aunt Sadie said, 'Can't you drive no faster?'

I kept jumping up and down with excitement, because the only places we ever went to were church, the garden to pick vegetables, the store, and to feed the pigs down near the river.

'Look. Look at that big Ferris wheel! Wow. I can't wait to go on that. And

all those other rides. Gosh, there's so many. And look, cotton candy, hot dogs and everything. Even corn on the cob!'

I was just about to bounce through the hood of the car when Mommy said, 'Hush, Charlotte, don't get too excited now.'

Franklin spoke straight into the windshield: 'This ain't your beach.'

'What do you mean, it ain't my beach?' I said, in a voice full of tears.

'This here beach is for the white folks. You ain't allowed in it.'

'But, the water is for everybody, isn't it?'

'Yep,' Franklin said, 'but everything else done been made by these white people and bought by them and they don't want you to have it.'

'Mommy, I don't understand.'

'Well dear, it's just like when we came here on the bus and we stopped and you wanted to go to the bathroom. You ran ahead of me and I had to pull you out of the one you were in and take you to the other one. The one for us. The one that said COLORED PEOPLE. And you remember the water fountain? That had a sign on it too: WHITES ONLY, so you couldn't drink there and I had to give you warm water from the bottle I was carrying with me.'

Franklin then announced, 'Look over yonder. There's your beach.'

I craned my neck and hung my little body from the car. I couldn't see anything like the beach we had just passed. Then I saw it: a mean, sandy stretch of land with a tiny figure pushing a cart in the distance. The cart held a sign. I squinted and finally made it out: 'Hot Dogs — The Best and Only Treat You Gonna Eat!'

The Audi swung to the right and started down the narrow, twisting road that led to Dad's and Mom's house. The pines had grown taller and thicker and seemed to be leaning into each other and 'shuushing' as if they were whispering secrets. The river was still muddy and sluggish. I could smell its salty sourness and it made me so thirsty.

Maybe it was going to be alright; Mom would give me a big, cold glass of lemonade, the glass moist in her hand as she placed it carefully on the coaster. Then she and Dad and I would sit around and share our stories.

14

FUNERAL

AS I stepped out of the car, my heel sank into the soft, red earth. The wooden church, with its once white slats, now bearing patches of brown and grey, stood amidst gravestones, some leaning earthwards, as if the message they carried was too much to bear.

The organ swelled, and then receded, as I made my way down the aisle. Faces familiar, yet changed, stared back at me. Other family followed: bigger, older, wearier. We found our places in the pew.

The preacher stood tall and resplendent in robes of black with red flash. Arms beating like wings, he urged the congregation to stand up as we sang, *Precious Lord, Take My Hand*. The casket was gleaming with silver and enveloped in color: pinks, whites, reds and yellows. Flowers in the shape of hearts, circles, horseshoes and various other configurations festooned the front of the church.

Rising, the choir began its wail and whoop. Sopranos swooping and swaying upwards, basses searching deeper and deeper, the sound swept over us and I fought back the tears. I didn't know Rose that well, it was just the church and the music. The music did it every time.

After the service, we filed out into the back of the church. Franklin kept hissing something to his wife, Sadie, but I couldn't make it out. We all congregated by the huge space that had been made for Rose's casket. The whispering whirr of the levers that eased her into her eternal home was the only sound to be heard until Franklin shouted: 'No!' He seemed to be trying to lean into the gravesite and one of the undertakers quietly took his arm to guide him away. Franklin jerked his body away from the man and said, 'I have to talk to her. I gots a story to tell.'

Everybody was shaking their heads murmuring, 'What a shame. Poor man.'

Then my cousin Eddie said, 'Oh, go on and let the man talk, if he want to. It's his momma. He can do what he like.'

People looked astonished and sucked in their breath, but they reluctantly began to turn their backs on Franklin and head towards their cars. I could hear his pitiful, faltering voice beginning to fill up the air. 'Mama, I don't care. I got to tell what happened. The whole thing. How it was. I just can't keep it in no longer.'

Franklin :

Sadie had big bones and a tight smile. Her hair was soot-colored and wavy. She wasn't no pretty thing, though. She had a jaw-line that jutted out and her eyes was real small and pinched. Her skin was a yellow color, like an almost-ripe banana. I always wanted one of those cream-colored women, with that mix-up of white and Indian. We all knew they was the prizes.

We got married in 1938. Sadie was eighteen. Man, I remember that day, 'cause them damn shoes I had on was killin my feet. Couldn't afford to buy no new ones, so I borrowed my brother's and his feet smaller than mine. Matter of fact, that suit wasn't fittin quite right either, but it was a real deep blue and I was gonna show these people.

Sadie looked almost soft and pretty that day. She had on an ivory dress she made herself — satiny, shiny stuff with a little veil across her face. Her sister, Estelle, just took the show though. Lord, that woman was somethin to look at. Her complexion was like a rosy pear, with warm eyes the color of mink. Oh man, you could just melt lookin at her. And her hair was so smooth. Lord, she looked just like a white woman. And when she spoke, well, that just did it. Man, I woulda followed her anywhere.

When I saw her outside the church, she smiled her polite smile, but I know she weren't studyin me at all. I mean, I got these buck teeth and nappy hair and be darker than my brothers. I wasn't in her world. She was lookin for a brighter horizon.

We settled in and all and Sadie started havin children after a while. We had a fat little girl. Then, some years went by and we had another girl. Well man, this child was golden. You hear what I'm sayin? Golden. Hair was golden, face was golden, everythin golden. Now, I know they gotta whole lotta mix-up in that family, but this here wasn't comin out right. Where we be gettin some golden girl from? Man, I knew somethin was twisted up here.

Anger come all in me. God, but that golden child, was some kind of beautiful, though. Seemed to be glowin all the time, with that silk hair and that buttermilk skin. And her eyes. I forgot to tell you about them things. They was blue man. Blue. Now you know I had me a treasure in my house. A real gold piece.

Papa Mason, my daddy, had himself a real gold piece too, even if just for a minute:

He was watchin the dust dull the shine on his new brown shoes and feelin the wet wind against his coal-black face and stringy black hair, when they came. She come at him, with her three friends, all of them fallin. Fallin this way and that, on and off the road. Kicking up a cloud no matter which way they went.

He wasn't tryin to inch into their lives or anythin, just wantin to show some decency and concern. His mouth started workin before his mind and the words was bouncin off them trees. They came boundin back sayin: 'Why you be so big-mouthed?' Mind answerin: 'Well, they looks like they need a word to help them from fallin and all.' Even he felt like fallin as the air choked up with the smell of alcohol. When they got closer, the smell and them was one. The worst was on her knees, with all that sunshine hair tryin to mask that red and white face. The other three tryin to hold up sunshine. Mumblin and slippin on the grass, they brown hair be pressed to they dull, wet faces and they smiles be fixed like a minstrel.

Flap, flap, his tongue was steady hittin his lips. Felt his whipped-up excitement, like the Lord had opened a special gate that he could just walk right through. 'Good evenin, ladies. Look like you havin a big difficulty here. I think ya'll oughta take that sick one to the nearest doctor. She don't look like she can be goin on much further. Dr Bedwrack live just up yonder; big grey house with a red door. Can't miss it. Ya'll want me to help? To carry her?'

Ain't nobody answer. They just thrust they flat, hard grins in Papa's face. They eyes was tellin a different story, though. Finally focusin, after eatin up everything in sight, them eyes looked straight at Papa and said, 'blood time.'

When Papa Mason come home and told his story, everybody in the house turn granite. As he was talkin, he could feel his hot self turn to a cold wind. A wind bitter in its search for revenge and a place to settle. He had to find it. A safe spot.

Mama, I was doin OK, then things just started to happen. 1955 was the year. Henrietta was fourteen then. Hair down to her waist. That's when somethin break up inside me. Drinkin all the time. Drunk. Metallic be in my eyes. Bright, blindin world, no shadows. Yellow flash.

That's how this woman come on me. Yellow flash. Right in my face. Had on this blonde wig and put her head all in my eyes. Leaned over me and called the bartender: 'How long I gonna have to wait? Till they builds a skyscraper in Tidewater County?'

Twitch started it. In my eyes. That blond business. What a colored woman want to wear that shit on her head for? Shakin. I was loud: 'Why don't you serve this here lady, man? Want me to bust up this place?'

She was turnin to me. Put her hand on the bar. Lord, gold bracelets — must have been five or six of them things. Rings too. Flashin that shit. Some hot and cold come over me.

I'm comin towards her, sayin 'It's all right, sugar. Daddy love you, you knows that.' I just keeps walkin, walkin. Seem like a forever thing. I there, right in front of her. Grab her arms. Hard.

'What the hell you think you doin, Mister?' she said. 'Let go my arms, you crazy nigger. Ain't this somethin? Buy you a drink and then think he can just mess you round.'

The sweat was pourin. Wish somebody would take all that bright light away. Close the curtain or somethin. Things be yellow-bright everywhere.

What that yellin? I looks and my hands be round this woman's arms.

Made marks. 'So sorry, Miss. Don't know what I be doin. Please forgive me. Bartender. Another drink for this here lady.'

I walked on out of there and peoples just be callin me I don't know what. Ya'll don't understand. It was the gold that did it.

The old pick-up groaned down the road. Where was I goin? Couldn't go back to the house with all them steamed-up feelins the family had. Needed some quiet space. I just kept on drivin. Then this face come to me. An old, black twisted thing, with a mouth screamin and as big as the moon. Somehow, it looked like Grandpa, who was born a slave. He spoke as if he thought the world couldn't hear him. My ears was ringin:

somethin come over me in that tobacco field. i tired of bendin down and comin up to get nothin. been slavin for these bastards for so long; too long. and what they did to my martha. lord. that child in the big house. lookin like my wife, but not lookin like her at all. all them reddish-brown curls. lord.

i could feel the shadow near and movin closer. a scissor-edged voice take over me then: kill the mother-fucka. kill that overseer. kill him. I rise up and strike with my fist and swing the big tobacco knife. he duck and kick me hard. down, down and up again. that pink-red face all in mine, messin with my life. he winnin now, got that other pock-faced bastard with him. feet be all over me. a sole kiss my face and that be it. beat again, and again, and forever. beat.

Grandpa. Grandpa please come back. I need to talk to you. This golden thing. I didn't mean. Had to get rid of the sick. It come all over me so much. You knows what I mean. All that red-flame, all that steel, all that sharpness. Want to get back at them. Take that shit and ram it down they throats. Make them know that burnin black thing too. Make them know it strong. Make them know it rise up. Make them know it a fire.

My eyes was so blurred. I couldn't see the road no more. I had run the damn truck up in a field somewhere and my clothes was wet and smelt so strong I could hardly bear it. I kept drivin around in this field, circlin, circlin, my mind flyin out through my ears. Oh Lord, Lord, where I be goin?

Seein Grandpa helped me through it all then. Sadie be busy runnin this place and that, makin new shifts with red and golden flowers on it and smilin that mean, pinched smile.

It don't matter to me, though. I through with her. We moves to different rooms and life be easier since I don't have to be with her in bed. We ain't never really wanted to be next to each other anyhow. Just did what we thought the world expected us to do. I must be grindin my teeth at night or somethin, 'cause my mouth and gums be hurtin so much every mornin when I gets up. But I forgets about that soon 'cause I gotta new woman now. Well, sorta new. She the one I met in the bar and hurt her arm and all. I kept apologizin to her till she calm down a bit and now I think she sweet on me. At first, I still had some trouble with that thing on her head, but now it looks right nice. In fact, it be one of the prettiest things I done seen in a long time.

TENTATIVE STEPS

WHEN I reached the house, it was already full. Voices were knocking up against one another, lips smacking. There was food everywhere: fried chicken, ham, potato salad, green salad, shrimp salad, macaroni salad, collard greens, cornbread, dinner rolls and about five or six cakes, each vying for pride of place with the gloss of their icings and decorations. And booze: a liquor store strewn across the adjoining table.

I slid my way through the crowds to the table heaped with all the food that gave me solace and found a plate. Standing next to me, six-foot and cream-brown, stood my cousin Eddie. I had already warmed to him for what he did for Franklin.

'Eddie,' I said. He looked, and then looked again.

'Charlotte?'

'Yes.'

'I hardly recognised you. You've cut your hair or somethin.'

'Yes, the hair is cut and the something is I've gotten a bit older. How are you?'

'Oh, alright, I guess, if anybody can be alright in this sad-assed place. Sorry, just can't deal with most of the folks 'round here. Everybody is in everybody else's business and busy rushin to try and outdo each other. So borin. Ain't nobody really interested in anything that is interestin. Only Darlene. She's trying to do somethin to help these people. Tryin to get some of our land back.'

'Really?'

'Yeah. But that's a long story. I'm sure you'll run into her now or while you're down here. I notice Trevor couldn't be bothered comin. Held up in Hollywood, I 'spect. Mr Big-Shot movie star.'

My mind flipped back to Trevor. Must admit I did look around to see if he had come and felt a slight, sharp pang of disappointment when I realised he didn't show. Beautiful, smart and self-absorbed, that's all he could offer. When he was young though, he was capable of sweet love, tender moments. But self-hate and hunger drove him to crueller touches and indifferent embraces. We had something once, but it was too convoluted and involved to unravel; at least not now. In a way, I was glad he hadn't come. As I glanced around the room, it seemed I had enough to deal with, as it was. I had to lean in hard to bring myself back to Eddie: 'Nice car you got. Pretty color, too.'

'Thanks, but it's not mine. I rented it.'

'Well, rented or no, Charlotte, better ditch that thing, 'cause there's no way it's gonna stay in the driveway for more than two minutes. Need a garage for that baby.'

'No one would steal it, would they? This is Tidewater County, not the South Bronx.'

'Almost one and the same, now, just more trees. We got whatever you want, just up the road. Drugs be everywhere around here. Listen, I don't mean to be rude or nothin, Charlotte, but I need to get away. Just hearin all these folks chatterin and talkin trash gets on my nerves.'

He gulped his drink, wiped his mouth with the back of his hand and put his plate down.

'Come and look me up sometime while you're here. We'll talk some more and you can tell me what's shakin with you. OK? So long. Catch you later.'

I could see Eddie stride out to his car, a nice, new, metallic dark-blue Chrysler Imperial convertible. He looked like he had a handle on life. He waved as he slid into the seat and smiled the most brilliant smile I had ever seen as he sped down the road, music blaring.

Eddie:

Man, I ain't never smelt no sweet pussy like this before. Every time I take my hand from the wheel and put it cross my face, here she come again. All over me. Whew-wee. And I'm on my way again.

I like flyin in my car, with the sounds from the radio taking me up and stretchin me out at the same time. It's like the radio is in my heart and the music stream right through my veins. And I'm like in the middle of the air. Know what I mean? Not up in the sky. Not flat on the ground. Just coastin right there in the divide. Yeah. In the cut. And dippin in the dust. White dust. You know baby. Some good shit. Man. Got to be doin somethin round here, or be fuckin out your mind. And I sure as shit ain't goin down that route. Oh no, baby. Too many by the wayside. Too many.

People be thinkin we ain't into nothin way back here, but this place be poppin if you know where to hit it. Jammin and freakin and all. Hell. I'm havin a good time. Cruisin and gettin into it. All them fine honeys. I'm a bad mothafucka and ain't nobody tell me different. Shit. I'm way cool. I'm one fierce dude.

I sure do hate it when this shit wear off and I got to come down, though. At least I know when to stop. Some cats be takin that little crystal and they be gone for good. Yeah man, and sweet sisters too. Shit be too sad to think about. Suck your dick in Malmeyer's window for some crack. Out of hand, baby. They be callin this place Crack City now. But ain't no little piece of white rock gonna crush my world. I been tellin you what a good time I'm havin and all. Well hell, I be up in the high sometime, but it ain't all the time. But say look baby, you got to put up that front, keep that smile, and lie that lie to get on. Right?

It used to smell honeyed round here. I don't know. Maybe it didn't, but it seemed like it. Momma cooked a lot then, and we always seemed to be near Momma, who was always near the stove. Food be on the table, in the plate, on the counter, in your mouth. Food be everywhere.

Just like now, but it's a whole different story. Now, you be rollin along the road and it come up at you from every direction. Wham: McDonald's, Burger King, Wendy's, KFC, Cap't Smith's Seafood, Taco Bell, Somebody's Pancake House, and a whole buncha new shit whose names I can't even remember. After a while, it don't matter what the fuck you be eatin. It all taste like the cook don't care. And after you finish, you always be wantin somethin and don't know what it is.

In the beginning, when I was younger, I thought I knew what I wanted. Get smart and stay clean with my vines. Get out in the world and be somebody. Not stay around here. I was really tryin, you know, but I finally got hip to what was truly goin down here, and from what I was hearin, it wasn't much different anywhere else, so …

I went to school and all. Teachers were dumber than me. Check that! Found out that all the folks that had the lowest state exam marks would be sent down here. I heard that some of them didn't even pass. That's some real shit, ain't it? Let me tell you, those folks was some kinda thick. Man, school was like sittin in a room full of sludge. I be so bored. I could look at Cheryl's titties and my dick wouldn't even get hard. Yeah. At first I was into readin and writin and findin out about the world and shit. But these lame-ass teachers sure as hell wasn't into me. They didn't give a flyin fuck what I was interested in, what I thought and most definitely where I might be wantin to go in this life.

I worked a lot on my own, you know. Readin what I could and tryin to have it all settled in my mind. But some stuff was just from another world and nobody was explainin the shit. So, I still dream about books and learnin and stuff, but basically now I'm more into things I can get my hands on.

The line tugged hard and I almost folded over myself and fell in.

I pulled and pulled and it flicked and flashed and bent me again. Finally, I reared up, it flew out and was mine. I had me a big-mouthed bass. Brother said he caught a sturgeon once. Four feet of fish. I never saw it. It was before I was born. But I was born to this. This river. These fish. These trees. Pecans fallin, a blue-jay blindin with its flash of white and the blood-red of the cardinal. Dusty old roads and green-brown against blue, blue-grey and black. I felt right out here and with it. The land in my hands. The salt-warm splash slidin between my toes. Some kinda pull here. Some kinda sweet. But baby, you can't live on a pecan and a bit of perch, now can you?

You see, feel like some hard air be pushin against you and you just gotta go with the deal. Plus, after you figure out the shit, the game whitey be playin and all, you don't really give a damn no more. I mean, you got to look good, right? Well, what else is there here? You know, get the gear and shit. Nike Air, the black leather, all the threads necessary to hang. Might as well, 'cause I can't see no way outta this trip. You just got to hustle to be with what's goin down. So, I do the legit shit and some not-so-legit shit too. Can't be livin on what your boss be givin you. You wouldn't be able to feed a parrot offa that tired shit. Don't nobody live off this land no more, 'cept some ol confused folk that don't know that the world done gone and changed up on them. I'd rather be duckin and divin and doin a little of my high shit than be standin on the street with a sign at my feet sayin: 'work for food'.

Man, I just let my eye fly across this land. It used to make me heave up with such a happy feelin. Loved to be out in it. Some kinda swellin come through me. Spendin hours smellin trees and flowers and shit. Yeah. Y'all think that's dumb, huh? Well, I liked it. I love this ol fucked-up place. I bet it wasn't always like this. I mean, they put that landfill right in the middle of the joint. Supposed to be far away from the community and shit. Well hell. You wake up in the morning and that smell come at you so hard, make you want to spend the rest of the day kissin the toilet seat. And what do people think all that garbage be doin to the river? The soil? It's a real mothafucka. Sometimes, I can feel somethin throbbin through my shoes. Life down there. Somewhere. Bangin. Furious. Ain't my fault the shit so messed up. I don't know what happened.

I remember when I was young, got this feelin that everybody be pullin together so as to get somewhere in life. You know. Nice house. Nice car. Nice job. Nice clothes. Nice children. Nice. Nice. But the thing flipped up on us. People don't seem happy with 'nice'. Hold up! Ain't nobody ungrateful. I'm glad I got what I got and all. But people be walkin round here with great big sockets for eyes. Burnt-out. Drugs or no. Getting all this material shit — the 'thing' thing. It just ain't makin it. There's somethin missin. People confused 'bout who they is. I mean, you know, history and shit. I think we ought to get a grip on the shit, but this country ain't into no history, baby. It's now or never. For sure.

I keep thinkin, 'Do I want the prize?' I mean, this big, big house surrounded by trees, shielded by dogs and some live fences. Do I want to have to unlock so many locks, undo so many alarms that by the time I get in the fuckin place I'm too tired to appreciate all the shit I've accumulated and can't remember what it is anyway? I mean, what is this American dream all about? Look like it's a sweet dream for some and for the rest of the suckers out here, a nightmare baby. A nightmare.

Hell. My head be hurtin from tryin to figure all this shit out. What I need to do now is stop by my house, get all my gear, slide back into my car, turn up the sound, let that melody make me mellow and burn up the road gettin to where I want to go. That's right baby. You got it. I'm goin fishin.

REVELATIONS

WALKING back into the room, it seemed that all the voices had risen. Hilarity and hysteria began to intermingle. I saw Mom and Dad on the far-side, Mom looking slightly pained but wearing that sweet smile, while Dad drank the dark-brown liquid quickly, made a loud 'agh' sound and began moving his hands in rapid motion while talking with his mouth meanly twisted in one corner.

Funerals always got to Dad. The drink took precedence at these wakes. The more Dad drank, the further away my mother's eyes would travel, until he was in his world and she in hers.

As I looked for somewhere to sit, I heard a squealing, jerky sound. Accompanying it was the noise of things falling, loud bangs. I couldn't figure out who and what it was, until I saw this shining form coming towards me. It was Cousin Sister with so much fake gold jewelry on her that it seemed almost impossible for her to stand upright. There were strand upon strand of necklaces, one fighting the other for prominence. Then her arms echoed her neck. Her ears bore huge cut-glass rectangles with dangling gold bits and even her chest had hope pinned to it.

'Wow, Charlotte. You lookin great.' Cousin Sister sped forward into me, her arms clasping hard around my ribs.

'When, when you get here? I didn't see you at the funeral? Was you there? I got a car now. You got to ride with me. Want to go now?'

'Uh, no, not now, thanks. I really should stay and talk to some of the folks here. Sorry.'

'Well, you be 'round, won't you? I come by and take you for a ride. Tomorrow?'

'Well …'

'OK. Tomorrow, 'bout two o'clock. I'll see you then. Boy, we gonna

27

do some talking. I got so much to tell you. Grandma Rose dead now. Wonder how Daddy really feel? He'll never tell me, though, so it will always be a mystery. That's my Daddy, mystery man.'

I looked in wonder as Cousin Sister wrenched herself away from me and dived into a piece of cake she saw on the table. She pushed the cake into her mouth without barely swallowing and kept pushing and pushing. Her hunger seemed prodigious.

As Cousin Sister and the afternoon worked themselves into a frenzy, I felt the need to get away from that recurring question: 'Ain't you married yet, girl?'

I pushed through the clatter and found myself on the back porch. Seated, singing an unrecognizable tune, was my cousin Henrietta, Cousin Sister's sister. She was big. Very big. She had gained at least forty pounds since I saw her last. Her blond hair was now brown, but as she turned to face me, those blue eyes were as piercing as ever. And strange, angry marks, like little rings, dotted both her arms. Frowning and hauling herself up in a knot, she said, 'Who are you? What you want?'

'Henrietta, don't you recognise me? I'm Charlotte, Preston's and Estelle's daughter.'

'You that stuck-up man's child? I remembers you now. Your momma a good heart, though. I could hold her hand all day. Do you hold her hand?'

I stumbled on words trying to hide the shock. 'I, I, well, yes, sometimes, not always, though.'

She was not the little girl I used to know. So changed was she that I could barely remember how she was, but, by God, she was certainly different from the person that rocked in that chair now. She seemed to be mumbling and when I called her name, she didn't respond. The words were becoming a little more audible as she carried on, but I felt I had better leave. Or maybe I wanted to leave. As I eased back into the house, it seemed trees were on her mind.

Henrietta:

the trees was agitated. i seen them like that before, but this time they was bendin all over one another, thrustin their face in my window. and screamin. they kept whoo whooin, cryin and makin so much noise. i couldn't understand why they was bein so wild and mean. They already knocked over dr simpson's car and put a hole in the small shed behind the garage. they was carryin on, snappin at one another, barkin and such. i got so excited i started screamin with them.

then here come that woman. she make me sick. always pokin her head in my room tryin to get into my business. and that smile — like a whip across her face. i know she don't care nothin about me, just tryin to irritate me. but i don't let her. i just laugh and laugh loud — don't answer no questions — and finally she let me alone.

this time she just stand there, talkin about storms and such. Her mouth be just movin so fast and all these words be comin at me, like i'm on a firin line or somethin. her mouth seem to be ahead of her body, it was movin so fast. the room was fillin up with so many of her words that i couldn't breathe.

i don't know why people always got so much to tell you, like you don't see nothin, think about nothin. she never asks me what i be thinkin about. she just be tellin me what she be thinkin about. i don't care what she think. she a hollow log.

mouths been movin at me for so long, that i can tell when one is gonna cut me up. i can tell them sharp mouths a long way away. momma had a sharp mouth. i don't know why, 'cause all her sisters had soft ones. ones you would like to see move, holdin sounds close and makin them warm and open. i don't think momma's mouth always like a knife. when i was little, i remember it being a cushioned bowl that i would put my fingers in. but momma start slicin me up. stabbin me with them words so cold, like steel. i fix her though. i use more than words. i pick

29

up the blade one day and make it shine near her eyes. she move away from me then. but she call that white committee group to tell me mumble-stories and carry me away from the shinin blade. i been on the move ever since.

seem like momma always be fixin herself — pattin hard, like she gonna fall apart or somethin. and be lookin in the mirror with a question on her face. i wonder if that mirror ever answered her question. she sure asked it a lot. sometimes her eyes put holes in other people's faces. especially pretty women's. she put holes in their faces for days. and her sound when she speak to them be thin and stingy. but when she speak to daddy, she just wipe him right out the room. he live upstairs at night, not downstairs with momma. he used to spit a lot.

he liked to smile when he saw me, though. kept talkin about my hair and eyes. i think he really liked them, sayin they was golden as the sun and blue as the sky. i thought they was funny though. ain't nobody round here look like that except those white committee peoples with their mumble-stories.

i didn't like golden, i liked brown. i used to buy me big jars of grease and slide that stuff all into my hair. my hair be slick-down and shinin, and it be gettin darker all the time. now it be real dark brown and so greasy that no matter how many times i wash it, it always stay real close to my head and shine, shine.

before it got real brown, though, daddy be all tangled up in it. talkin about shirley's curls or somethin, he always had his hand in it. watchin his hand in the hair, mooin and moanin. he said it made him so happy, but it sound like he sick to me. momma say he better leave me alone, but he say ain't no harm and the child like it. ain't nobody ask me nothin about likin. it used to make me feel wormy or somethin. crawly. like things all over me. don't know why though. maybe daddy's voice goin too deep into his body make me feel like he want to bury me.

he always got that low-voice when he come real close and ain't nobody around. he be busy lookin at me — my hair and all. then there was that day when he be all over me, his eyes hungry and watery, where he go all up under my dress and things.

i be standin in momma's bedroom, making her bed. she had that peach bedspread on with the little soft bubbles on it. i like to run my fingers over the bubbles. then daddy. then daddy come in. seem like his teeth be shinin, shinin. oh lord. he walked. he walked towards me. he walked towards me with his hands. oh lord. oh lord, my god he was strong. so strong. low-voice. low-voice spread through me. split my body. up and up and up. pushin through. pushin through and through me. loud. loud. so loud: 'you mine now. you might not have been before, but you mine now.'

daddy made me strip the bed and wash the sheets. made me wash myself too. blood be everywhere. i seen some of it when i first got up and it was bright and shinin, just like daddy's teeth when he finished with me. now it dull and dark. look like mud.

when momma come home, i try to tell her about daddy's teeth. she don't want to hear about it. i surprised she can't see it. it be so clear to me. they shine so bright, they light up his whole face.

i keep tryin to tell momma about the teeth and all, but she be busy goin out with all her men friends. always be going somewhere. by now, daddy's teeth was blindin me. that's when i wanted momma to see the shine so bad, i picked up the shinin blade and put it in her face. then she called them peoples to come for me.

i found some more shinin though. i come to get used to it. they always be puttin me in the old, sick-green room. they puts me on a cold table and straps me down. they put these little metal plates on each side of my head. then the shine come. sometimes i go right to sleep, but most times i be seein and feelin more shine than ever before. my whole body become electric wire. i on fire. explodin into all these pieces. i be screamin from a big red spot with flames comin all out of it. nobody shine like me.

they said i was gettin better a while back, but now they don't know. they took me out of that sick-green room place and now i lives at dr simpson's. see, he own all these rooms and houses. i think there be five houses in all, and a whole bunch of us stay here. it's nicer than the sick-green room place 'cause we got our own curtains and chairs and things. my sister say the family help pay for it. i guess that's why it look so nice.

they let me have a friend. his name thomas. he come to visit me a lot. he try to have that split-me-up stuff like daddy had, but i don't let him. so, he got a new game we play. thomas smoke cigarettes. so he bring in a whole pack and we get started. he light up the thing then he press it on me. at first, it hurt somethin terrible and i didn't like it. now, i used to it. plus, i love the tip with all them lights. anyway, he do this on my arms and legs and things. last week, he do somethin different. he take that red spot and put it on my pussy. ooh-wee, that was some feelin. i felt like i was shinin in the sick room again, only more. i told dr simpson about it. he got real shaky and started coughin somethin terrible. said somethin about 'we'll see'. but he didn't come to see us when we was doin it last night.

my sister come by sayin she want to take me home. i don't know though. momma still there and i don't want to see her. sister say all the mens is gone, but i don't believe her. plus, she don't never listen to my stories. even when she come to visit. she just say, 'child, go on away from here with all that mess.' who want to be with her? daddy might as well be dead, i never sees him, so i don't have to be split-up no more. but thomas and i, we got each other here. i can see the shine with him.

we talks about lots of things and then we plays that game. sometimes, i just can't wait for the red spot, goin all into me and turnin me into fire. i'm all ablaze and shinin. i'm lightin up the whole world.

Big Fun

SHAKEN after being with Henrietta, I really wanted to get away. Dad was gesturing as if holding a rifle, with a raised voice that made Franklin step back against the wall, while Mom stood there traveling in her mind. As I tried to make my way out of the house, Mom's eyes found mine and pleaded: 'Please don't go.' I thought I might find some peace and cold water in the kitchen, so pushed my way through. Seated at the table, with a mirror placed in front of her, sat Aunt Sadie. She turned, but her smile was not a welcoming one.

'Charlotte. How you doin?'

'OK, Aunt Sadie. How about you? Lovely wake,' I said, as I fidgeted with my dress.

'Must have been an awful lot of work.'

'I'm used to a whole bunch a work, but lots of people from round here helped out. Did you get enough to eat? Help yourself. There's plenty more.'

I remembered Aunt Sadie always had food on her mind, although she wasn't as fat as I had pictured her. More muscle — brawn, really. Could knock you out without thinking about it, I guessed.

'No thanks, I'm full to bursting.'

'Well, if you ask me, you look like you eat air for your meals. Child, you need some food in that little belly of yours.'

'I'm really not that thin, honest. Anyway, I feel better this way.'

'Well, why don't you sit yourself down for a while.'

Somehow, I knew this wasn't what she really wanted me to do.

'Thanks, but I just came for some water.'

'Help yourself. There's some cold in the ice-box.'

As I opened the refrigerator door, Aunt Sadie said, 'You ever talk to yourself? You know what I mean, you be thinkin about something and then it just all spill out of your mouth. Like, if you hold it in, you just burst wide open.'

I turned, without speaking, and Aunt Sadie tossed her head as she said, 'Oh girl, must be the funeral, me talkin this way. You go on back inside and maybe Cousin Sister will bring you by tomorrow. I'm kinda tired to be talkin now.'

'Of course, Aunt Sadie. Tomorrow.'

As I left, I heard Aunt Sadie turn on the radio. There was singing, but there was a voice grating against the song. It raced against the beat:

Sadie:

I kept lookin in the mirror to see if it had changed me. But it hadn't. All that was different is that I hardly had hair anymore. And it made that ol jaw-line of mine seem to stick out more than ever.

But that dress was somethin. Nobody could say different. Them seams was so smooth. And I designed it like nobody else could. The way it draped over the bodice and all — it was a strikin thing. I could design things like this in my sleep. Coulda started me a business or somethin. God knows I wanted to. But where I be gettin money and all? Bank sure wasn't lendin no half-Indian money to start no business. In fact, they laughed at me, them tight-jacketed men in they silver stripe suits. Thought I was some kind of dreamin fool. Just 'cause I didn't own a whole lotta stuff. I had me some land though, but they didn't even pay attention to that. Like land weren't nothin no more. Can you imagine?

Franklin didn't pay no mind to my designin neither. Ask me why I be wastin so much of my time messin with that machine when they be so much work to be done in the field and all. Said to him, 'You go on and do it. You ain't got nothin else to do but bother me to death. You go on out there and do it.'

Not that I don't care about the farm and all, but I loved to be creatin all this pretty. Some of the womens round here would ask me to run them up a dress or two, but my ol relations just didn't pay me no mind. Kept talkin 'bout, 'Think she better than the rest of us. Can't be workin in no field.'

I sure know the one that thought she was better than the rest of us, though. That be my sister Estelle. So damn pretty make you want to spit. Gone and left everybody. Livin up North with that skinny-ass, yellow nigger who think he be God's gift to womens. He couldn't do nothin for my left foot.

Well, anyway, I got so tired of Franklin messin with my head and yellin at me, that I seem to change up all of a sudden. Just like that. It was that real hot summer of 1943. I wake up one mornin and I say, 'That's it. I'm gonna feel good somehow or another if it kill me.'

Then the memory hit me:

I look in the mirror and starts brushin my hair real hard. It be halfway down my back. I puts this greasy stuff in it, tryin to make it shine more. I presses my hand against my head and then pushes some of the hair backwards to make a big wave. Saw my ol big hands and them fat fingers. The nails be down to the quick.

Hear a knock, then the screen door screech and a man yell: 'Howdy. Anybody home?'

I wipes my hands on my dress and go towards the door. There be Mr Green. Somehow and another, he look better to me than he ever did before. Seem to have a kinder sound in his voice too. 'Nice day we be havin. Not so hot as to make you crazy.'

'Yes', I says. 'Breeze keep you from goin wild.'

Then he says, 'I saw Sister out front. Give her some candy. Where Franklin?'

'Oh, out yonder in the field somewhere. Then he said he goin over to Rooster's. He be gone most of the day, I guess.'

Then there be this silence. I could hear a mosquito agitatin the air like it was flyin inside my head. Seem like we was both swallowin up all the air in the room. I feel faint then. Mr Green take off his cap and wipes his brow. The cap be stained all the way up to the mesh part at the top where he be sweatin. We knew then that a cool breeze wasn't gonna be enough.

Times be so different after that. I be all freed-up. And I feels so pretty, so wanted and all. I just up and started flirtin with all these different mens, and they be smilin at me like I a princess or somethin. Lord, it sure made me feel good. I loved that wash of warmth that spill over me when they be lookin at me with diamonds in they eyes. Even my sewin go by the wayside for awhile.

My life be busy then. Make-up and hair and fingernails and girdles and even new shoes, though they most times hurt my feet terrible. Got that Sears and Roebuck catalogue and went to town. Then one day Henrietta go sour. Sickness in her mind drape over her like some willow tree. She be bellowin and talkin about Franklin's teeth and some kind of shine. It was all I could do not to go along and get twisted up with her. Franklin's eyes be like slits, and he keep so much tobacco in his mouth, that when he say somethin, you don't know what he be talkin about. It was then seem like a whole lotta dust settle inside my head and I couldn't get nothin clear no more.

Seem like Henrietta was talkin about Franklin messin with her body. I just can't believe that. That man don't really seem all that interested in sex in the first place. Used to go to sleep most of the time. Maybe it was just me he weren't interested in. No, that can't be it. It just that he be dull in the sexual parts. I should know — I be his wife. But Henrietta keep on insistin. I just can't understand it. Maybe she feel she should have some and ain't gettin none. I sure know what that do to you. But even if she all stirred up, she too young to feel that bendin over urge. Why in hell she want to start this here mess? I keep tryin to visualize Franklin and all about what she say, but I can't. It just ain't a believable thing to me. I just refuse to believe that the man I done married would want to do the thing she say. I got to figure out how to keep this child quiet. I got enough to close my eyes about when it come to Henrietta. I sure as hell don't need no more.

So what if I had me some mens while I was with Franklin. I don't care what anybody say. They made me feel like I was breathin again. I got so excited about the whole new thing after a while, that I guess you could say I went too far. I ain't never had no white man look at me like that before. We's had a new doctor in town. He have this blonde hair and his eyes be the coolest blue I ever did see. They was like an icy pond and they pierced right through me. At first I was shiverin and I was sure that I hated this here man. But it was his voice. Came from some warm, sure place. Place that couldn't be shaken, no matter what. I ain't never had no white man be speakin to me like that. Just wanted to curl up in that voice and be safe forever. My head buzzin. Skin stretchin towards him. Yes. God forgive me. I wanted this man to put a hand on me, stroke me, make me feel good. It all happen so fast. In a flash. I knows I had no business, but he was the tenderest man I ever met. Or, it seem that way at the time. And he said I was beautiful. Beautiful. I can still hear his voice sayin it over and over: beautiful, beautiful, beautiful. Then the baby come.

It was a golden thing. Just like him, 'cept the face look like me. Peoples be whisperin and cluckin they teeth like hens. I started talkin up the white part of the family, sayin, 'You know how funny these genes can be, child. They pops up when you least expect it. I bet her hair go brown soon anyway.'

'Yeah,' they say. 'I knows what you be talkin about …' 'cept they eyes be so wide open they takes up half they face.

Well, I didn't want to do it, but the child just got worse and worse. Then, when she pick up that knife, I knew we had to make a big change. Yes, I called them mental peoples. I didn't have no choice. That child was gonna kill me, you hear? Well, we all has to look out for ourselves, right? She been in there so long now, I don't even know who she is. She big and fat and talk a whole lotta gibberish. Come to think of it, so do her sister, but at least she can travel through her little world alright and don't be shovin some shiny steel in my face.

My life ain't no big fun anymore. That stopped soon after the Henrietta thing. Sure, I tried to keep on enjoying company and all, but the air seem to be all dry and the mens hands feel like pine bark. And they just seem to be sayin the same ol stupid shit over and over. Don't seem like none of 'em got a brain in they head.

Ain't much revvin my motor now. I's old and tired and don't seem to want to see nobody. The peoples round here done talked so bad 'bout me and my family, I just closed up shop. Far as I's concerned, Tidewater County done closed up shop too. But at least I can say I had me a grand time. Yes I did. At least I think I did. Sure I did. It was some kind of wonderful. That is, until this mess done start.

But you can't be worryin about no mess forever. Sister done asked me to move in with her and all. I suppose it bears thinkin about. I guess I'll take my rockin chair and sit out on the porch and consider this thing. And besides, feels like there's a nice breeze blowin.

ALL I WANTED WAS SOME CANDY

'ALL I wanted was some candy.' Cousin Sister said this, staring straight ahead as she accelerated — then slowed — all within thirty seconds. 'I know I ain't supposed to be drivin', but I does it anyhow. So what if I ain't passed my test yet. Ain't nobody notice around here anyway.'

How I wished I hadn't listened to Eddie and had kept the car; now I was trapped.

Cars behind began to honk. People cursed. Sister stared straight ahead and kept talking. 'Charlotte, you remember Bubba Lane?' Trying to laugh, some strange, strangled sound leapt from her mouth. Her head jerked back and forth, as she said she could just see him — that big old fat, butter-colored man with his moustache and balding head.

'He had a whole lotta candy in his shop. Remember them Mary Janes and the hot cinnamon balls? I liked them ones that was light purple and tasted like them tall flowers with the big fannin-out leaves at the bottom. What they called? Oh yeah, I know now. Irises. He used to give me some of them for free.'

She licked her lips like a windshield wiper. The car leapt, only to crawl suddenly again.

'Yeah, he sure liked them ladies. That good-lookin Mr Green, he was a real ladies' man too.' With her mouth pulled tight against her teeth and grunting as if in pain, she doubled up on herself and the car slid sideways.

'You remember Mr Green? He had that blue pick-up and he always had bags of candy in it. I sure liked his candy. He would come and visit Momma a lot. She would just be smilin hard everytime he come by. Daddy wasn't around much then. Always seemed to be goin' somewhere in a hurry. Somethin' about a blonde bar.'

Then a hush, except for the pump and release of the accelerator as Cousin Sister let the past come to her mind.

Cousin Sister:

You could hear the gravel crunch. The dogs howled and spun around each other. I let all the chicken feed fall to the ground and tried to wipe the dust off my feet with spit. I could hear Momma's voice from way back in the house sayin, 'Just a minute, I'll be there in just a minute.'

I was brushing back my hair when he parked his truck out in front of the house. I was trying not to jump up and down, but I could taste them things.

'How you doin, Mr Green? Nice day, ain't it. We got corn comin up now, and some real nice butter beans. You want some?'

He brushed right past me and said, 'uh huh.' His voice was all watery and weird, and his eyes seemed to be closed although they was still open. I stuck my neck into the truck, then turned and put my hand out. I just knew he had some for me. But he didn't pay me no mind.

He was in the house now and Momma was laughin funny. It was high and sharp, like she was scared to relax into her sound. I was all inside that truck. I looked everywhere. In the glove compartment, under the seats, even tried to open the hood of the car. I wanted some candy. I could just taste it. All that sweet, sticky all around my teeth and me trying to get it off with my tongue.

I thought, well shoot, I'm goin inside and ask him for it. I went on in the kitchen, but I couldn't hear nobody. Momma had cleaned off the table and the red oilcloth was all shiny and stuff. She had put the lid on the slop-jar over in the corner and picked up all them pieces of wood that always be laying round the stove. Even the floor looked real clean.

I went on into the parlor and kind of peeked before I stepped in. Nobody was talkin or nothin. In fact, there wasn't nobody there. I wanted some candy. Where was they? I heard some sounds from the next room, where Momma stay. Why they in there, with the door closed? I wanted that stuff so bad, I wanted him to give it to me, so I just went on in … Momma beat me for the next two weeks.

We cruised quietly in a fug of heat for a while, then Cousin Sister slumped into the steering wheel. Sweet silence was gone when she said, 'Momma had her a whole bunch of boyfriends, you know.'

The car was burning up. Hot. Acrylic shag seats itching, like long, fuzzy fingers. Sister was talking fast now, spewing out words, tumbling over sentences.

'You remember Dr Thomas? My mother use to go to him every week. When he change his practice and move to Roanoke, she use to go all the way there to see him. Momma and Daddy didn't even sleep in the same bed.'

She was laughing so hard by this time that her foot kept jumping off the accelerator as if it was on fire. She sputtered and howled as tears creased her face.

'My sister Henrietta be in a space walk and Momma and Daddy don't even know it. They don't notice nothin. Be in their own locked-off world. Can't nobody get in.'

I remembered when Henrietta's feet were on the ground. She was so alive, so aware. We used to walk down the sticky tar road, smacking mosquitoes, talking about color and sound all around us: discussions lasting hours about the variance of shade in green leaves, how the sun and shadow changed the intensity of a rooster's crown and what color the river really was. How she wanted to paint, to leave Tidewater and see the brilliance of the world. Her mind always probing, taking in all she could of my life; a life for her that seemed so alive and full of promise.

She was so sensitive, though. You knew she could see the starved look in her mother's eye, the melancholy wash in her father's. Could feel frustration raging underneath their cool exchanges, and recognize the neediness enveloping both.

The memory of those unclouded afternoons was snatched from me when Cousin Sister screeched, 'You ever get beat a lot? I used to get beat real bad. All the girls would get it. We be seein too much of everything. And hearin. We be under the house listenin to the springs jump up and down. We was wise to a whole lot. We knew too much.'

'Henrietta be almost blinded by what she be seein. Always talkin 'bout somethin in her eyes. Then when she used to come home from the mental hospital, she keep sayin, "Don't let Daddy near me, don't let Daddy near me."'

'I think Momma put her away because she had a whole lotta information and she always kept talkin. Yeah, that's what I think.'

We turned off the main highway, entering a parched, private world. No people to be seen, just old barns and new brick houses, standing isolated. The road thinned, twisting around an old, slow-moving river.

Sister turned as we approached the grey, wooden house, neglected and needing paint. There were a few chickens scattered in the yard, pecking at the dry, cracked earth. A broken tractor was near the back of the house, rusted and leaning to one side. The screen door had a rip in it and was flapping in the frame. The garden, about half an acre, was desolate. Grey-green shrubs and leaves pushed forward haphazardly, brown ones echoing the grey.

'When you get to the house, guess you be wonderin where my stuff is,' Sister said. 'I done taken it all to my new place. I told Momma she gonna have to leave here and live with me. But she don't want to. She and I might get to talkin about things. That might not be too good. You wanna go in? She sure would be mighty pleased to see you.'

Aunt Sadie was now standing at the door. As she approached the porch, the sun spilling onto the steps, she seemed disorientated. She pulled back, frowning, and looked as if she might return into the house. We came closer and Aunt Sadie finally spoke. From a great distance, a voice said in a hush, 'So nice to see you.'

She looked into my eyes for a scant second, squinted, then turned on her heels. Picking up one heavy foot after another, she hummed her way back into the house. Sister said, 'Momma got some lemonade. You thirsty?'

43

'No thanks,' I said, backing away as I licked my lips. Sister went forward into the house. She said something to her mother I couldn't hear and Aunt Sadie's voice jumped a decibel. 'No, don't be askin me that mess. Go on away from here.'

We both sat in the car, listening to each other's uneasiness. Sister finally said, 'It's too bad if you can't go and see Henrietta. You gonna go, ain't you?'

I knew I was more than afraid to go, but somehow a muttered 'Yes' was forced from my lips.

'They let her out for the funeral and all, but I wants her to come home for good. She says they treatin her bad where she is. She say she got a boyfriend. She got these marks or somethin all over her body. The doctor say they's a reaction to the medicine, but I don't believe him somehow. It his mouth. All twisted up and tight. I don't know, but I'm gonna try and get her out.'

I said, thinking of those strange circles on her arm, 'Just take her out. If you all are paying, then she can leave whenever she wants.'

'Yeah, I'm gonna work at gettin her out. I talked to Darlene about it and she said to do the same thing that you say. I'm gonna do it. I'm gonna do it soon. I know I will. I have to think about it some to get it right, but I'm gonna do it. I know I will. I know I will.'

A CLEARING

IT HAD been almost a week since I'd last seen Cousin Sister. She was panting when I opened the door. She had on a see-through white blouse and a black bra and her stomach swelled under the pressure of the waistband of her skirt. As usual, the ropes of fake gold pulled her neck forward. Her arm rang out in dissonance, bracelets halfway to her elbow, as Cousin Sister thrust the book in my hand.

'Boy, you won't believe what she been writin. I wonder if this be the truth or somethin she be makin up. She could always tell some stories. You just got to read this now, Charlotte.'

'What are you talking about?'

'Well, I went to visit Henrietta and I saw this strange lookin book on her dresser. So when she went to the bathroom, I sneaked over and put it in the bag I was carryin. Did you see it when you went? Well, anyway, it had her handwritin in it, so I thought, Charlotte should read this.'

I took the black book that said, 'Journal' in gold writing across the front and opened it. Henrietta's small and florid script covered page after page. There was no capitalisation. Just words falling over one another, jostling for space.

'OK, I'll read it, although I don't really know if I should. Feels like an invasion, somehow. I didn't see it when I went to visit her the other day, because she was so busy showing me her painting. It was really very good. Have you seen it?'

'No. She don't show me nothin. She say I don't understand or ain't interested. I wish she had some interestin jewelry, though. Jewelry, now that's some beautiful stuff. How come you don't wear a whole bunch of sparkly stuff, Charlotte? You sure nuff got the money.'

'I'm not really interested in it. I mean, I like jewelry, but I'm not too crazy about diamonds and gold. I like semi-precious stones like amber, opals, garnets, that type of thing.'

'Well, whatever. I loves the sparkle. I'll be goin now. I'm gonna go downtown to Malmeyer's. Hear they're havin a sale on gold jewelry. Sure hope I can afford somethin. Wouldn't that be wonderful? Real gold, all over me, just sparklin.'

Cousin Sister turned and ran to her car. I could hear her stripping the gears as I began the first page.

Henrietta:

rip the book up. that's what thought shoot through my brain. shred and shred. let it fly off to some other eyes. some other head that could hear it and not know it lied now. it lied. yes. i be lookin out the window and ain't nothin i see be like this book called history. eddie, my cousin, bring it by and i be lookin and studyin and cryin and crammin. tryin to get it way-down meanin. what it really hidin underneath. what it be sayin. try to know why what it talk about be swept off the earth and this other thing put down we be callin life in tidewater county.

see. it say that a whole bunch of hundred years ago. wait. yes. 1608 or somethin, some white peoples come on boats called 'somebody be constant', 'godspeed' and 'discoverin', lookin for a new world. they come round to this place all dressed up in they crinkly hot clothes and start eatin and shootin and talkin a whole lotta trash mess. it say my peoples from way back then be livin by the river and doin good. whole lotta sturgeon. they be big fish. some peoples want they eggs. i member momma cook scrambled with some roe. also, it talk about them weavin some baskets. and huntin and such. elk, deer, turkey, muskrat. all kinds of what not. sound like we was just coolin out here and makin a life-song. but, like i said, here they come. mr smith be leadin them up river. they even say that princess pocahontas be savin his life cause her daddy want to kill him, cause he be so greedy. nobody seem to know why she want to save this little ol tired white man, but maybe since she princess, she could have him for a special playtoy.

maybe she want to make him do things for her, instead of her and her family doin for him. that sound right to me. anyway. here they come. and takin. not even askin after a while. all the green and yellow and pretty and plenty and happy things be happenin just go down the river. that be it. the river. that salt fresh curlin tongue. they river now, they think. be floatin on it and talkin some bent ideas. sayin yes when they mean no. sayin friend when they be meanin turn your back sucker. even if you don't turn, i'm wipin you out with your eyes buggin, and my gun poppin faster than your bright stick that fly.

my head reel up in a whirlin state. try to think of how all that lovely and peace and sweet thing be washed away and now we is all dried up. the river still be flowin, but sometime it just hardly be makin a mark: slug, swamp, and slow move.

i hear it though. talkin to me. yes siree. i keep tellin everyone but they just howl and twist. eyes be waterin up. some just get the head-shakes, like they hair full of bugs or somethin. anyway, can't nobody stand still when i talk about my conversations with the river. maybe they been hearin and talkin too. maybe too shy to say. ain't no doubt to it though. the river make excitement.

it say, 'watch out. i'm comin back fierce and tell my story.' it say, 'i'm gonna flow up so high and hard, the whole land be washed clean of sad and blood and filth and lies. my tide gonna be like a big sea. surgin. jump up and arc my back. fling myself into the sun. be sparklin.'

i get a thrill when it talk about sparklin. sparklin is a wonderful thing. i'd rather listen to the river and hear what it have to say than what a whole lotta peoples be tellin me anyway. specially momma and daddy. this river speak from a wide, yawnin place. place i been to with it. river know it all. the deep answer. me too. you can know if you listen. whole buncha voices liftin up. just singin. sweet water flow washin over. first a scream, then just a sweet, sweet water flow.

talk about sparklin. the star just left. charlotte. that woman be a bright ball in my life. every time come down. clean, pressed and pretty. well, not all that pretty, but pretty enough for makin a smilin face. colors swirlin round. dresses of pink. prints of lavender. reds, yellows and blue-whites. everything just spotless. bring a big bag too. full of left-overs for us. not blue-white, but not grey neither. we be prancin in her past, imaginin her present, and i knows both be shinin.

she a movie star. i knows it. i seen her in the pictures and on tv. she tell me, 'you must be craze.' she shift, then say, 'don't be silly.' but i knows she is. got a kindness in her face. a glowin that be used to peoples goin out to her, givin a spirit or somethin. sometimes a big curtain of grey come down over her face, but she push her hair like a bird wing arcin and she be bright again.

there been a clearin in my mind. i been readin a whole lot more stuff. that lawyer cousin of mine, darlene, always come by bringin the words. cousin eddie used to bring some, but he too busy speedin now. darlene words be thick on the page. hard to get down in. to hold up to the light and see the meanin. but i'm doin real good, i think. this history thing again. got my head huntin. so much they be sayin about folks round here that done left long time ago. i mean, the first slave person we know of in this here country come bang, right here on this big river that's part of ours. be an age before now. i member that date. 1619. and they say my peoples put outstretched fingers and hands full of corn and all to them darker peoples when they try to get away from that red-open back runnin. white man be screamin and got a whip. make em do a lot more than daddy make me do. even the mumble peoples at dr simpson's done stopped puttin me in the green room with too much blindin shine. that happen when charlotte come. i just want to say, blessins be to a star.

anyhow, they treats them folks bad. even badder than they treats my momma's first folks. her first peoples knows the land better anyways, so they just slip behind the tree and lose them peoples. then they be gettin together with the darker peoples who done flowed over to our river. our peoples be holdin arms and heads and takin the salt tear with the sweet night. be babies born. be pretty things too. i bet.

i be seein that some of the dark mens be fightin in some big war. revolutionizin, i think they say it was. the first president, washington, got some of them to join, though at first he didn't want to hear of that mess. he must have gotten scared of losing the thing though, so he had to ask them to come and get hurt for him. when they finish, they think gold pot. but washington and friends just push they face back in the earth with the red-cut runnin.

then there be a whole bunch of other mens. be big thinkin peoples and leadin folks. some of them name jefferson, locke and linnaeus. them mens had theories, you know, like 'life, liberty and the pursuit'. but they be split-hearted christians, cause they got a weepin-sick idea of who my great, great, great grandma be hookin up with. listen to this: they say that orang-outangs would be happier layin with her than they own kind. what this be? supposed to be foundin fathers. but I knows no monkey lay with my past peoples. they did. who they kid. talk about some age of lightenment. look like darkness to me. especially when them wives of the foundin-fathers, some susannah lady or somebody be lookin at them babies runnin round and be seein they husband face washed with the red-brown. sometimes be yellow curl, like mine, on them heads. must make hers want to bust wide open.

then there this other story be messin with my mind. this slave, he say he 1 out of 734 owned by mr 'c'. he be wearin all them fancy, hot hats and all them dress-up clothes just to drive mr 'c' up and down the river road. but he be chained to the carriage when mr 'c' keep him waiting while he in the house. his vines might be sayin somethin, but he didn't have no best of life. his horse did. mr 'c' used to bring that horse into that big ol house, right in the dinin room where he had him a silver bowl. bring that animal right up to it and let it drink clear to the bottom. champagne. you think that horse be happy drinkin that? it give mind some thought.

then theres more. this field slave, his name josh, he be drinkin somethin different. be beat and worried and full of nightmare. don't think he much more than baby. used to wet his sleepin place, dreamin bout them welts he gonna get. master say, 'you like to do that. well heres what we do.' he give josh this yellow drink come from him. in a pretty glass. but it sure must be terrible. i know josh head never be right after that and bet he can't even look at no lemonade.

i know these here people be watchin for a sign in this here blue black of they lives. i be crush-up hurt when i can see them raindrops fallin like glass and they hearts be bleedin in the river. but they the keepin-on kind. i know, cause i'm here.

this is somethin. our story. i don't know what his story is, though. who he anyway? this be our story and it be so excitin. why nobody know this thing? the jitteries comes over me when i be figgerin it out and i blows up with anger sometime and fly with the fury. but most times, i be expandin with the self. knowin that i come from fightin peoples. proud peoples. peoples who got the kernel of calm in them and an eye for an evermore.

TWO

Old Beginnings

I BENT down and picked up the desiccated earth. Dust covered my hands, my shoes and the sun spared no mercy as it singed my hair. After so many years of luscious growth, with Estelle and Preston working so hard, I found myself walking through my parents' defeated garden and into the cool green of the forest. There, a hush surrounded me: a kind of humming peace. The crack of a bough sent a blue-jay in flight, its snap making my heart pump. I took a breath and breathed in the scent of pine and river-salt, which calmed me.

Scudding sounds and flapping leaves made a chiming chorus, and their song lulled me as I stopped and sat on the trunk of a walnut tree. Finding some comfort in its old, craggy base, I tried to gather all the broken shards of my family's life and place them in a less furious place in my mind. Tried to slough off the past and believe that the future would right itself, but that hard seed of hatred just seemed to keep re-inventing itself. Could anybody in this place ever really look at the past and then look at each other?

Weighted with it all, my eyes closed as the wind began to stir. I didn't care and sat there as if pinioned. Thunder began to clap as if the gospel chorus had churned the congregation to a state of ecstasy. Smack-smack. Over and over. I was rolling with it, the boom making my head snap, the roaring hammering my ears.

The tree-tops bashed one another. A wail in the wind worried the flight of birds. The sky turned phosphorescent. I looked up through leaves as clouds scurried, trying to get away from something that seemed to be chasing them.

Good sense said 'run', but I was in something deeper now. Something coming from bitter earth, from saddened sky. From this land that, maybe like Dad, had seen too much, lost too much and knew that soon, if left without awareness and an acceptance of truth, would be no more.

The first one came from behind the tree next to me. Then they came from all the trees, up from the river, behind the rocks, folding into a huge army, marching, forever marching: brown with red, red with red. Blood a banner on their bodies. Arrows, hatchets, pistols, pellets, knives, ropes, chains, saws, manacles, machetes, rifles, cannon-balls and whips all whirled around me, beating the air with their fury.

Screaming, my eyes afire, I watched them heap hate on one another. Their arms thrust to the skies and then at each others' hearts. Swirling, from some circle of madness, they danced their death-dance. The wails rocked the roots of trees and then they began slowly to recede from sight, eyes turning to sky and limbs to loam. Soon, there was nothing but a hum, as the arms of the forest took them back again.

Tidewater County was talking to me, a confession of confusion and outrage. I knew that until all saw it, heard it, and made it their own, the blood-march would go on. Soaked from the sight of it, I clambered up as the swing of the hawk's wing showed the way to the clearing and home.

Home: that new, old place that echoed the fear and prudence of our New York days; Mom and Dad had run only to find a whispering version of their former selves. No problems settled, no words altered, no better clarity. Just less of it all: the clamor, the crowds, the smack-up-against-it reality. Here was a place of dreams, of nightmares. We found it hardened in the concrete of the city and running wild in the river and forest of this land. It played out all the years, hours and days of self-deceit and broken beliefs; reeled out, in flagrant display, all the merriment and intimidation, the happiness and horror. Silence seared by bird-cry and sunlight shielded by leafy trees, just aggravated a world which we all wished would go away.

Wincing as the screen door whined in protest, I pulled it shut. I knew I could run away from this place, but the place would never leave me.

As I sighed and slowly walked into the house, Mom's muted voice came from the kitchen:

'You're always disappearing. I can't imagine what you'd find to do, or see around here. Except for a snake or two, this is the dullest place imaginable. It's dead, really. Just plain dead.'

Surprise, Surprise

JUNE 1974, and the blistered road gave no mercy to the heat-wave. The old serpentine path swung and seemed to double back on itself, as the route sucked the tires in with each revolution.

Preston spit his words, 'You've got me in here and I'm never gonna get out. I know I wanted to leave Harlem to retire here, but God, what in the world have I done?'

Estelle said, 'Don't worry Preston, we're really not that far away. You're doing fine. Just fine.'

She turned and saw that his mouth was taut against his teeth. He looked as if he wanted to tear into something – or had – and the taste had been unbearable. She had to admit she liked it when he squirmed a bit, when he didn't have total control of things. But as the trees crowded in on them, and the little brown river turned to swamp, she knew that her freedom was like that river, shrinking and about to dry up.

The townswomen were all aflutter:

'Well, I heard he just up and bought that land. Paid with cash, girl. Put his money where his mouth was.'

'Mr Flash. Always comin down here in the summer from New York, showin off and gettin on people's nerves. Well, he's here to stay now. Lord, honey, what you think gonna happen?'

'Happen? Nothin. 'Cept we all gotta go around to the house pretendin we like him. But she's so nice. God. She always seem like such a good woman. Although, sometimes, I think she believe she one-step above and all that. Plus, child, I hear she one bakin fool. Anything you put in the oven that rises, she can make it taste like it come from heaven. Wouldn't mind that. Not too many folks around here be cookin anymore.'

'Well, maybe their comin down here be good for us all. Put a little life in this place. Or, at least, give us somethin to talk about, honey. 'Cause we sure needs some new gossip. Folks be so predictable. You know, I suppose that's what they'll bring us. Surprise, baby. A whole lotta surprise.'

The tree was growing through the window. Her heart stopped. Too much. It was all too much. A glance backward in her mind and she was in the long, narrow kitchen again. Where she stayed too long and worked too hard. And that was always before and after work in somebody else's spacious, accommodating and too-large-to-clean kitchen. But oh, those sweet, sour hours in that thin, bright kitchen. Where baby smeared spinach on the wall. Where porridge bubbled every winter morning. Where roasts and pies were produced and succotash simmered and was greedily savored. Where pots produced sheen and knives produced fear, especially after the two-day bouts with liquor and life.

It was this small space that was an ever-changing miracle, a hot-house of the whole thing. The tang, the taint, the temerity of the day-to-day. The 'this is possible, we can get through it, don't forget your boots' kind of courage and clutter that made up the everything of that beleaguered Harlem brownstone.

'Well, don't just sit there staring, Estelle. Get out and help me with all this mess.'

Jesus, he thought. So much growing around and into this place that I'll never get inside it. It'll be one hell of a long time before I can rest easy around here, I can see that now.

She didn't want to move. Ever. Never again in life. Just sit there, in that soft sunlight and dream a dream. Or remember a dream. Or the hundred dreams she'd had before she left this place. A dream of eating oranges everyday, every hour for the rest of her life, as she pulled the sap from the gum tree, softened it and popped it in her mouth. A young mouth so eagerly awaiting the burst of bitter-sweet juices spurting to the sides of that warm cavern, shocking it and making it tingle. Just at Christmas, only at Christmas, were oranges like this to be found.

'Estelle!'

Why did his voice always hurt so? It wasn't that loud; in fact, he had a lovely tenor song in it. But it didn't have – what was it? Some deep caring, some real truth. And where was the 'I love you no matter what'?

The branch sprung back and slapped him in the face. He finally snapped it, unlocked, then opened the door. There was no welcome here. Peeled wallpaper, dust settling on him with every footstep and cobwebs clustering on his eyebrows made his heart sink. Yes, he thought, I should have stayed in that damned, dirty city. Let the bastards rob me so they could hasten their death with heroin. Let the garbage fester all up and down the street 'cause the city don't bother to collect in Harlem. Let me keep on bumping into these women with all their damn children and ain't no man to be found nowhere. Let me ride that filthy subway jammed up against some two hundred pound prostitute that swears I'm trying to feel her up. Let me go to work and be less than a man cause I'm bowing to some stupid, white, fat-bellied, ignorant, son-of-a-bitch who thinks he's better than me and doing me a favor letting me work like a damn dog for him and he's giving me half of what I'm worth. And he just smile and pick his teeth. Yeah. Let me go back to all of that. The tears rolled and mixed with the cobwebs as he bent down and scooped up the dust in his hands. Let me go back to that in my coffin. And only in my coffin, Lord.

She had spent all her life running from this place. How did she ever get back here? She loved her people, very much, very much. But it was this land. This land, so dry now, so wanting, that made her weep. This land, this place was poverty, hard, hard work and indescribable emptiness. It didn't invite the world to it. It shut itself off. It didn't want anybody anymore. She felt it. Knew it. That's why she left. Had to find some kind of harvesting place. A place of plumage, of color. A place where thoughts blossomed and ideas grew. This was a barren space now. Tired. Had given up its soul long ago.

'I'm gonna do a whole lotta planting, Estelle. You wait. I'll fix this house up and plant a garden that will be a showcase. We'll make this the talk of the town. Corn, beans — oh yes, lots of beans and greens — collards, mustard, Swiss chard. You know. And melons, and squash, and … What color should we paint the house, Estelle? I think white with green trim. Nice, fresh and neat looking. It's gonna be alright. I'll work the whole thing out. And you'll be cooking all this stuff that I'll be growing and we'll have us a real life now. A real story-book life.'

Estelle saw herself bent over from picking. Gnarled fingers from cutting, washing, canning, frying, soaking, freezing. She felt the inner frame of herself fall in a heap in front of her. She looked at this new-old self. She screamed so hard her head burst. Except nobody heard it but her. All Preston heard was, 'Yes, dear. Yes.'

LAVENDER SEA-SALT

THREE faces just sitting there staring. You'd think somebody would want to ask a question or something. But no. The only sound was of stainless steel against porcelain, a slight slurp from a cup.

The whole thing was unbearable. Mom's strained half-smile. Dad's rigid neck and averted eyes. A human voice finally filled the air and resonated through the pristine, yellow kitchen.

'So, what are you going to do now,' Mom said. 'I mean, Charlotte, have you saved any money?'

A grimace slashed across Dad's face. 'Save. Her? Don't be ridiculous. No. She's got to have the very best. Only the finest of the fine will do for our little daughter here. Just look at these clothes.' He pinched my arm slightly as he touched the fabric of my blouse. 'Linen, isn't it? Linen!' He said it with a snarl.

'Well, where do you think I got it from, huh? You and your camel's hair coats, mohair suits and your silk ties so your Windsor knot wouldn't bulge too much. You didn't skimp any. Putting up a front was the important thing. Make people think we had so much. The apple doesn't fall far.'

'Listen here, Charlotte. I do have something. I've got a house, a car and a couple of acres of land. I worked long and hard for this, and I'm proud of it. What have you got to show for all those years of college? All that money? My God, your mother and I killed ourselves so that we could give you a good education. And what do you do with it? Paint pictures that nobody in their right mind would want to buy, and mess around in plaster or something. Calling it sculpture. Like some child playing in a mud puddle. I mean, I think it's nice to have a little talent and all, don't get me wrong. But when are you going to get a real job and have a real life? And what about a husband? There are plenty of good, black men out here who would love to have a woman who looks like you. Maybe they didn't go to college and ain't particularly interested in all that art stuff, but they could provide. You need a good home, some children. A decent life.'

How to explain that a decent life was more than two and a half cars, three children and half a husband? And what did my success mean to him anyway? All the exhibitions at Manhattan's most sought-after galleries, the reviews, the accolades — even the money. The suffering, the strain to put all of our lives, our history, into a work of pottery, a canvas. It was no easy task to be accepted in the art world, especially for a black person. It meant nothing to him. Jealousy reigned and he just refused to see and accept the truth of who I was: an independent woman artist, his daughter.

The air was dead. No open windows. Shades drawn. The whining of the air-conditioner. The legs of my chair scraped and shuddered as I pushed away from the table. 'I can't stand it in here any longer. I've got to get out.'

'It's about ninety degrees outside, darling. Where are you going to go in this awful heat?'

Mom's sweet voice was so loving, so sad and so resigned. It broke me in half.

Splintering the silence where confused thoughts condensed air heavy as the humidity, I said, 'I'll be back in an hour or so,' as I walked through the screen door and into the swelter.

The tar on the road bubbled. The pine trees, some needles brown from heat and disease, drooped their branches and dropped their growth. Pine and tar mingled. My foot pressed in.

Walking in a heat-haze, cars whooshed by and people waved. I followed a smell, a sea-smell that filled me full of yearning. This unnamed desire pushed me to a narrow, gravelly path. My feet crunched the small stones and made their mark as I pressed harder and picked up speed. The path then opened to a vast expanse. Tall grass leisurely guarded water. A river flowed — soft, grey-silver and

61

brown. Across its breadth, to the right of me, a chorus line of truncated trees, dressed in green flounce, lifted their arms in dance and celebration. This tidal river, calm and gently coaxing, was almost at my toe-tips. It lapped and pulled, teasing the ground beneath it with new configurations of sand and stone with every purl.

I bent down and smelt its brine. Took my shoes off and waded. Walked in its soft swirl and felt a place of peace. Eyes closed and wavering in the water, I felt her.

She stood, brown hair brushing her forehead, washed up from the river's edge. Her eyes blazed. Tied loosely to her wrists with garnet grosgrain ribbon, were small, pale-purple flowers. She carried an aroma of promise and anxiety. Sharp, acrid essence against a soft, heady smell. An ocean. An island. Gardens. Gardens and suffused sunlight. Lavender. Lavender and fear.

Her wet and shining body was oiled, burnished. Light-brown nipples tipped soft, rounded breasts. Her legs, lithe and ivory, met in a cap of glistening, curled fleece.

She sang, 'My sister of past and future. From country to country. My mirror, my blood-link, my love.'

I looked at myself, but not myself at all. I knew I knew her; knew she was in me.

She called. The river pulled. I stood and extended my hand.

'Take the lavender. Crush it,' she said. 'Crush it in your palm.'

I did. She did. Her fingers peeled away my limp, moist blouse and fluttered with the hooks of my bra. Released. Her hands began to circle my face, my arms, my neck, my breasts. Rubbing. Rubbing scent into me. She reached down and I was naked. Fully. We circled in fear. We circled in wonder. We danced desire. The sweat mingled with the perfume. The perfume with the sea-salt. Her body heaved, rising up. Mine an eddy to hers. A vortex, swirling. Her river flowed — on my hand, on my lips, on my face. Lavender and salt. Salt within and without. Buoyed. Lifted up. A dance through history. Sang languages of long ago. Tongues known and unknown. Through hot, dry land, green gardens. A sea journey uncharted. To fields. To forests. To river's edge. With memory. With license. With love.

Wet, my God I was wet. Soaked through. Even my hair was limp with liquid. Rubbing my hands across my eyes, I could see I was in the river. Up to my waist. Sitting there. Transfixed. I tried to stand. My legs wavered in the water. Bereft. Something was missing. Gone. The need gnawed at me. I felt so empty. Shivering, I left.

The sharp outline of the trees receded. It was beginning to get dark. Pull yourself together girl. You've got to get straight. Move it. Get home.

I ran up the gravel path trying to smooth my clothes down. Look normal. A few minutes after I reached the road, my cousin Eddie passed in his car. He waved and I hopped in.

His gaze lingered as his eyes took me in. I could tell he was puzzled. He spoke in a hushed, polite voice, 'So, how you doin?'

'Fine', I lied.

'Been walkin awhile, huh? Down by the Safe Spot?'

'Yeah,' I said. 'A bit too hot for it though. Think I should have stayed at home under the air. Keep cool, you know. This heat makes you crazy.'

'Sure do. I tries to stay still as much as possible when it gets like this.'

'Why do you call it the Safe Spot? How come nobody ever wants to talk about it?'

'Yeah, well, it's a long, nasty, complicated thing. Most people around here denies it ever happened, or just can't bear to bring the thing up. It ain't pleasant, Charlotte. It's really a shameful, horrible mess.'

'Listen, Eddie, I'm a grown woman. I can take it, whatever it is.'

'No. You's just a sweet little honey and you need to keep makin them pretty pots and pictures of yours and reading all them books. Ain't no reason to worry about some stained history of Tidewater.'

We drove the rest of the way in wariness. He said goodbye and seemed to emphasize his words: 'You take care of yourself, now. You hear?'

'Sure', I said. 'Sure.'

I slipped into the house, trying to get to my room before anyone saw me, but Mom was standing right in the kitchen.

'Good Lord, girl. Where in the world have you been? You look terrible. Your clothes are all stuck to you. And wrinkled. Even your hair is all messed up. For goodness sake! We're supposed to be going to Maude and Henry's shortly.'

'You mean those dumb people down the road?'

'That's not nice, Charlotte. You know they're supposed to be Daddy's friends. So, go wash up and change your clothes.'

'Just like when she was a little thing,' she muttered, with a smile crossing her face. Then she regained herself.

'Hurry up,' Mom called from the kitchen, as I stepped out of my soaked dress.

'And put on that nice new dress you showed me. You remember. You said it was imported from England. You know the one. It's that real soft purple color. Lavender.'

SUPERMAN

THE OLD house sat far back from the road, looking as weary as its inhabitants. A blue turned lifeless grey, its door held a female figure with a brightly-printed apron:

'Well, hello ya'll. Just come on in here. Me and Henry sure is glad to see you.'

I stepped up on the cinder blocks that led into the house, walked towards the living room and immediately felt faint from the heat and the fusty air. When we entered, Dad went straight over to Henry, clasped his shoulders and laughed. He said, 'Let's sit over in this corner and let the women-folk do their talking by the dining-room table.'

Mom and Maude kept smiling and saying, 'Mm, mm.' Finally, they both sat at the dining-room table as Dad announced that maybe I would be comfortable seated in the chair nearest the door. I sat, obediently, only to realize I was almost on top of the black-bellied stove, stoked and on fire. Heat fixed me, between the sultry blast outside and the stifling, pungent air within.

I continued to stay seated, although I was melting from the heat and burning up inside because I was still listening to my father and trying to please him.

As I wrestled with heat and decisions, Henry's voice rose to a whoop, 'Yeah, Preston. That man sure nuff raped his daughters. Two of em. Ain't that somethin to get ahold of? Ain't nobody done nothin 'bout it, neither.'

Everybody sat up, tight faces with voices battling their minds and each other. In the midst of the clamor, I struggled, my words clogged by the approaching nausea. 'Please excuse me. Must not be used to this weather. I'll just go outside for a little.'

They looked up, Dad with disdain, Mom bemused and Henry and

Maude a mask of grins. Their eyes glazed over as they bent back to their animated talk and dismissed me as if never there.

The grounds were barren and uncared for. Their pick-up truck was a medley of rust-brown and red. Two hounds scampered under the stilted house, whined, then rested their heads against the cool, damp earth.

I walked around the back and found an old folding chair. I propped it against a gnarled pine and began my war against the mosquito. As I smacked and swatted, that staircase, those trees and that gravelly, vexated voice jumped into my mind: 'Get in the woods, bitch.'

I was back there again; always traveling to this point. It seemed as if it would never leave me, this moment that burst upon the present without any warning and snatched away the day, even the week. A murky mirror at first, it cleared, sharpened, then slashed my whole world to pieces.

Mrs Whitworth, the house-mother, opened the back door of the college dormitory and stared. Her face a mask of calm, alarm flew from her eyes. Her gaze started at my shoes, then up to a twisted, wrinkled skirt, until she reached the blouse, torn, half done-up and the frame of terror that held them. 'Charlotte,' she said. 'What happened?'

Lips moving, sounds sputtering, I begged to be let in without explanation. Sitting in her grey room, book-lined and lifeless, the world of an hour ago rolled out.

'No, no, no! Why do you insist on not following the rules. There are ways of sculpting that you must master before you can go off with your own ideas. This is not acceptable. I want to see something correct first thing tomorrow morning.'

Ice caressed the outside of the studio, as the heat from the inside made it fight for its life. Then came the steamy tears running along the length of the window. The sun had long gone, even though it was only six on a December evening. The icy grey from the outside mingled with the diffused yellow of the room to give my immediate world a deep melancholy, a huge sweep of sadness.

I gathered myself together, gave an anxious glance at my 'correct' project, grabbed my belongings and dashed out of the room. Slipping on ice, I raced to get back to the dormitory before supper was finished.

There it was again: the dilemma. Which flight of steps to climb? Both started at almost the same point, so why were there two? I decided to take the second one, as a shadow flashed on the first. Preoccupied, I ascended the wintry, wooden steps and grieved about the project I had to abandon. I was deep in argument with Mrs Ramsey, my art instructor, when the shadow jumped right beside me. I flew up each slippery step as quickly as I could, with feet fast on my heels. As I was dropping books and fleeing, I felt a cold, sharp insistence. The knife stopped my feet as my mind raced for a solution. Within seconds, my voice found its courage:

'Listen. You don't want to do this. It's like doing it to your sister. You see, I'm black. Come on. Please don't do this.'

With his tongue grazing the inside of my ear, he said, 'I don't care if you were my mother, bitch. Get in the woods.'

The forest and graveyard stretched beyond sight. The trees, dressed in their winter white, were frozen in disbelief as we walked further upon a chilling, unwelcome carpet, the moon our only guide. The ice and twigs crackled as we made our way into the wooded area. The entire expanse was pitch-black, with no lighting coming from staircase or dorm, so the forest absorbed us, scowling and secretive.

My feet began to move faster, then broke away. I was running, running, hitting branch after angry branch that struck my face and lacerated my legs. Then my arm was snatched and jerked backwards. The cold steel pierced my neck and a hot, hissing voice said:

'Listen. This is a knife, baby, not a gun. I could just run it across your neck, like this, and can't nobody hear it.' His hot, sick-sweet breath was like a thick fog against my face. I placed my numb hand against the trail of the blade and sighed as my frozen fingers ached and began to turn blue-black. Yes, a silent death. That's what it was. Knife or no knife.

He was exacting. Everything had to be just so, or it was done over and over again. He wanted a lover that night, he said so, not just a body to *rape. Painstaking precision was on his agenda. Words were whispered in my ear, 'I love you, baby', to then be said by me repeatedly, until the right inflection was reached. 'Move here,' or 'touch it there.' Each part of me that I had to give away was rehearsed until the final performance was perfection in his mad, muted eyes.*

When his precise production was over, he stood and asked me for money to buy cigarettes. I knew then that death could come for not having the exact change. I reached for my bag, found my wallet and peered inside. No change at all. Just large bills. I said; 'Take the wallet. Take everything. It's OK with me.'

He paused and grumbled as his face began to contort. Then, as if a lit jack-o-lantern, he beamed, 'OK, that's just fine. But I want you to promise me something. You'll meet me in the exact spot tomorrow at the same time and I'll be back with your change. Promise?'

'Oh yes. I'll be here for sure. I promise.'

He scrambled down the slope, then paused. Cupping his hands around his mouth, he yelled, 'If anybody asks, tell 'em that Superman was here.'

With that, he ran and was eaten up by the night.

Superman came on time and was descended upon by a swarming dark-blue mass. Next to the police, he seemed vulnerable: a slight, eighteen-year-old, brown-skinned boy, with big, black, petrified eyes. They said he usually worked with his brother. I was lucky, they said.

When it was all over, I glanced at the surroundings. Lights magically appeared along the two staircases; trees and shrubs were chopped down to stumps. Little mini-buses scooted in and out of campus. The university was clean and clear of any incrimination.

Then the inquisition: Did I meet him at a party? Must have enticed him, knew him before. Black people like to hang out together, you know. The police precinct stank of stale sweat and was filled with cold, blank faces. The sergeant hissed between twisted lips of sarcasm, and said, 'No-one will believe you, you're not hysterical.'

My lawyer, the district attorney, wanted me to spy on students in my dormitory to see who was taking drugs. He said my calm demeanor was his reason for the request. The trial, the newspaper reporters, the vodka, the sleepless nights all boiled into one painful knot. The overheard conversations of some black male students inflamed the wound.

'She coulda fought him. Can't believe no black bitch let him get away with that. Wonder who she is? Ain't but nine or ten black girls on campus, anyway.'

In response to 'What they did to my baby', there was a lawsuit: the Rodgers against the University, for lack of security. It disintegrated in our attorney's office, as the money we payed him was risible against the might of the college. This little gullible, black family that was told they had a good chance of winning, watched as those odds became oblique, then faded away altogether. One afternoon, wanting to rip up that shiny, cheap blue suit of his, I roared in the lawyer's face:

'How much did they pay you? How much? How much to help destroy the efforts and dreams of a hard-working, naive, black American family?'

And then the family finally crumbled on that night at the dining-room table. As each swallow continued to saturate Dad with whisky, his spiraling cry went from 'my angel', to 'you whore.' Because I had decided to please a rapist and save my life, the world seemed intent upon killing me.

I heard scrambling and shook myself back into the moment. Mom and Dad were opening the door, laughing with a queer nervousness. As I approached, I could hear Dad's puffed-up voice saying to Mom, 'That's why I like to come here to see Henry. Now he knows what a great man I am. Knows all that I can do and have done. He just called me Superman. Yeah, that's right. I'm some kinda Superman.'

HEAD-TURNER

MOM was resting, the heat squeezing most of the life out of her. I went out into the garden, grabbing the few little sad beans that had defiantly sprouted against all odds. Shriveled tomatoes dropped their pained faces toward the dry and wanting earth, and corn stalks waved in the air, fruitless and drooping. This was the worst summer memorable. No matter what, the rains would not come. Or if they did, they pounded the earth with such ferocity, that the drops just bounced off and made their way back to the clouds. What happened to the peach tree, that generous giver of sweetness, and all the musk melons and watermelons? The stately rows of beans: lima, wax, string, butter — all gone. I know Mom was relieved, though. At least she didn't have to get up at three or four in the morning, to stir that huge pot that needed two rings on the stove. They had an industrial-size freezer, anyway, as big as a sarcophagus, filled to the brim with everything from the garden that Mom had frozen. No need to worry about food. Dad made sure there was always plenty, no matter what the cost to Estelle. He had no intention of going without. Ever.

As I approached the kitchen, I could hear Dad's voice booming. He was on the phone with some friend of his. I think he called him Buster. A smile ran straight across his face and a dance swept his feet in one direction, then the other. Great excitement filled his every movement. He was so involved with his conversation and the world he was spinning out, that he didn't even notice me walk through.

Preston:

Man, I like my women pretty and my pies sweet. I used to cook a whole lot, but I realized that was women's work. I had no business in no hot

70

kitchen. Of course, when I first went to New York, had to make me a living somehow. That was just some temporary stuff though. I planned to hit Harlem and hit it hard, even if it was the Depression. Hang out with the Ellington band, the Basie boys. Get some of them fine high-yella gals and promenade all up and down Lenox. I felt like a million dollars walking down that big, broad avenue with some fine chick on my arm. The brown tips of my spectators was shining and the white part was glistening. When the sun was out, made your eyes hurt to look at my shoes. Parted my hair in the middle and kept it pressed down. It had small waves, almost like a white man, but just a little too fuzzy and wild. Smoothed some of that Duke pomade on it, slipped on a stocking cap at night, and in the morning, well, I was cooking with gas. Lots of people told me I looked like Rudolph Valentino. Now, I didn't mind hearing that at all. I knew I was a head-turner.

The first one was Sarah. She was such a soft, sunburned color. The brown had some red in it. Long, thin legs like a gazelle; black hair hitting the small of her back. Sarah: the teacher who lived down the road. Bright eyes, bright mind, and beautiful. Loved her. Walking behind her. Mumbling, tongue-tied. Couldn't cut it. 1929 and I was only twenty-two. Had no words to woo this one. Desired her. Too dark, really. That wasn't the plan. Going backwards. Had to go forward. Get the lightest one; the woman who would have those children that could slip by, cross-over into that world of plenty. I was fighting myself all inside. Crazy about Sarah, but had to suck all that desire back and try not to let it burn me alive. I knew I was losing to gain. But I decided then and there if I wanted to be ahead of the game, I had better just slip on that white wanna-be mask and join the circus.

Estelle. She was standing near the far wall, talking to some old tired-ass black woman. A lovely sight, she was. Such a beautiful face. Almost like an angel. Creamy, apricot color with big, brown eyes and sort of auburn hair. Real good hair. Soft, loose waves down to her shoulders. Some strands kept falling in her face. Slow, lazy, almost like she was far away somewhere, she would sweep those strands aside. She stood out. She was in the crowd, but in her own world. I knew it had to be beautiful, 'cause *she* sure was.

My feet were moving me and I didn't even realize it. Gliding, I was almost at her side. She looked up, gave me a sleepy smile and let her eyes linger for a second. My heart was standing on its own.

'Dance?'

'Why, yes.'

I put my best foot forward and guided her around the slick, mahogany floor. Chick Webb's band was pumping, and some short, real fat, wire-haired woman was singing. That voice could make you melt, but man, that face make you want to run. But, what I had in my arms! This was it. She looked so white, I asked her what she was doing in Harlem. She laughed at me, shook her head like that was the dumbest question she had ever heard and said, 'I live here'.

Lord, this had to be mine. All any black man (or white for that matter) could want. I could feel myself stretching about ten feet as I pulled her close and saw the children. All beautiful. All white.

I knew Estelle's people didn't have anything good to say about me. Jealous. Hah. I didn't give a damn. I had done all this. Me. Preston Rodgers. Let them talk, with their old weather-beaten houses and their rickety cars. My car gleamed. It was a brand-new 1975 Chrysler. I bought it when we first moved down here and the sheen was startling. My house was a show-piece, in and out. A real jewel-box. I was Preston Rodgers and I'd done it all by myself. Of course, these younger ones were doing all right, but they had better chances than my generation. When I first come, folks around here my age didn't have anything except some false-teeth sitting in a glass and a sun-scorched brain. I even had a garden. Everything was growing. The earth was some kinda dry, but I put a trough through the field and then I'm selling stuff to the supermarket. They so jealous around here. They are. But, I'm like a white man. I'm a doer, a go-getter, a money-maker. A mean man of business.

I'm my own man now. Make my own decisions about everything, not answering to anybody. People come from all over Tidewater County just to look at the house. Plush, metallic-colored carpets, golden brocade chairs and couch. Gorgeous white bedspread and wood-work shining so hard you jumped back to see your reflection. I re-upholstered most of the furniture. Made all kinds of closets for the bathroom and kitchen. Just about rebuilt the entire house. Although everybody hissed and hollered about 'Oh my, this is just magnificent' and 'How did he do that all that by himself?' I knew they didn't like me. They were green with the thought of what I could do. I lowered my head a bit when the compliments flew all around to show I was a modest man. But it was a great thing I had done here. A great thing.

'The king will rest now.' That's what I thought when I eased myself into that big, all-embracing chair of mine, with the foot-rest that raised when you leaned back. After three or four years of work, I was the king and this was my castle. God, Estelle and I beat our bodies bloody for the land, the house, the glory. I seemed to swell inside, to grow larger because of it. But Estelle seemed to be shrinking. And puffing. And quiet. And just too damn far away. She knit all the time when she wasn't in the kitchen. And talked all the time. Not to me, not to anybody, really. Most of the time, it sounded like a low hum. Just mmmmm mmmming, forever and ever. I asked her who she was talking to, or what she was saying. She would look at me with wide, doe eyes and murmur, 'You just wouldn't understand'.

I remember when we first met. I had to sit in the parlor of her brownstone, hat on my knees, while some fat, ol snuff-chewing landlady kept creeping in to see if I was behaving properly. Well, I couldn't take that nonsense for long, so I asked Estelle to marry me.

We moved into a real, fine house right in the center of Harlem. We lived on the top floor, with a little, shriveled-up brown skin woman and her quiet, skinny, nappy-headed, milk-white husband on the bottom. That place was my first show-piece and we had some good times then. Of course, when I first got married, I found it hard to get used to the idea, so I just stepped on out that first night and didn't come back for two weeks. And guess what? That woman had the nerve to leave me. Yeah, she had left the place. But I found her. I knew just where to look. Went to her friend's house. Eileen. Big, big breasts and hair no longer than a minute. Knew she was crazy about me, but I can't stand no woman who ain't hardly got no hair on their head. Anyway, Estelle came on back home and we settled on in.

Man, then we had us a ball. Or, I did. Estelle would usually go to bed after the party began. All them women came to see me anyway. But I had to give it to Estelle though, when it came to cooking. Man, that woman could put the pots on. Except, all she ever seemed to want to eat would be them damn lima beans and corn. Succotash, that Indian dish. Sure, it was good, but all the time? Anyway, music would be playing half the night and sometimes the parties would push themselves through into the daylight hours. I would be the center of attention, with the women just fawning all over me. Yes, a grand time was had by all.

I tried to really settle down, but that roaming fever always took hold. Plus, there were all these women who were just dying to be next to me. I didn't want to deprive them of all this goodness, now did I? And work. Well, there really wasn't anything that was worthy of my talents. I just couldn't keep doing these short-order cook jobs and the only other two-bit jobs they allowed a smart black man to take. I know, I didn't go to college or nothing, but I had some friends who had all kinds of college degrees and they had them sorting and delivering mail at the Post Office. I knew I was destined for great things, but that mountain just seemed so high, no matter how far I jumped. So I just took my skills around to the community. Upholstery. That was my main thing. Did up couches, chairs, you name it. Beautiful work. Word got around fast. Also, I could change a size 42 jacket into a 36 and nobody would be the wiser. That's how I had one of the best wardrobes in Harlem. Of course, I had to do that steady thing too. Work for the Man, from 8-5, in some lousy factory, or hotel. One job was pretty nice, though. At least my baby thought so. That was the Windsor doll factory. We made the most beautiful dolls in the world. And the costumes: silk, lace, all kinds of fabrics. All pretty as a picture.

Speaking of pretty, here she come. Charlotte. My one and only. Now that little thing with all that black hair on her head stopped me right in my tracks. My brother was talking about her navy blue eyes. Sure, ain't nobody got navy, but hers were such a dark brown, it was really hard to tell for sure what color you were looking at. Well, I settled down then. Worked all the time, just so my baby could have everything. When she got to be about four or five, I used to take her around to some of the bars to show her off. Yes, I'd hoist her up on that bar and she would just start reciting all kinds of stuff. Sometimes, she would even sing, 'Jesus Wants Me for a Sunbeam'. Man, I thought my chest would burst wide open.

As the years went by we noticed that Charlotte loved all that scribbling and painting. Always talking about color. What color is this, that? Lord, she could ask some questions. In fact, she never much bothered with those beautiful dolls I brought home. Said it was no fun 'cause she couldn't change them. All she could do was look. Why couldn't she have one that cried and wet like everybody else? I just had to keep reminding her: she wasn't everybody.

'Man, I had better get off this phone. Yeah, it's some story, ain't it? Boy, I got loads to tell. Why don't you come by sometime next week and I'll make you weep and laugh all at the same time. I know, you ain't never heard nothing like it. Well, wait till the next time. I'll blow your head off.'

MOVING BACKWARDS

WE SAT huddled up together on the sofa, turning the pages of the album. Mom's eyes were misty with recollection. 'Look at you here. You must have been about four then. Had the longest old legs I ever saw and the biggest feet. That was the only year you were skinny. After that, everybody called you pleasingly plump.'

I stared at this knocked-kneed little girl with two fat, brown braids, pleated skirt and a white beret, clutching her shiny bicycle, breast puffed out, proud as she wanted to be. What had happened to that self-assured, bright-eyed person? Was she still lurking somewhere within me, clambering to get out?

'Oh, look at this one.'

I bent down and saw my Mother standing next to this man with a smile that would light up all Manhattan. Tall and square-shouldered, he was a figure of striking good looks in his uniform. They were standing in front of a train and my Mother looked happier than I ever recalled.

'Who is he?'

'Oh, just some nice man I met when I was going to Virginia one summer before you were born. He made sure I had a good seat on the train. He was so nice.'

Mom's eyes became wet and hazy. She turned away from me towards the window.

'Tell me about him.'

'Oh, there's nothing much to tell, really. You'd be bored.'

'No, I wouldn't. Oh, come on, Mom, tell me.'

'OK, but it really isn't all that interesting.'

As she spoke, I knew that I was fading, as an old life came new again:

Estelle:

Roosevelt had just become president and that summer was my first escape from Preston. I was on my way to Virginia. He said, 'Madam. You don't have to sit in the colored car with your maid you know. You can sit in the white cars at the front of the train.'

He had a red, round, flat-topped cap sitting on his head at the kind of angle that seemed to say 'I talk a fine line, lady. You interested?' And I thought to myself 'Why, yes I am.' And that red looked so good against his face. His skin was the color of wet sand that had little gold flecks in it from the sun, like I remembered from Bucksloe Beach. And his teeth, they were white white. As white as Mrs Perlman's linen that I had to wash and iron all the damn time.

I said, 'Oh, I'm happy here, thank you. There's no problem at all. She's not my maid. She's my cousin.'

I remember then that Alice shined up at him. A bronze Elizabeth Taylor she was. But I noticed when her lips went up in that half-moon, the corners pinched up real tight. Made her face look like she was trying to smile for the dentist.

His mask cracked wide open then and that iceberg smile just went into melt-down. He laughed, I laughed, Alice laughed. We were making some music now, our laughter like singing. But, the song carried the underside of it all too. The wariness and the fury. So, if you listened real close, it sounded more like some of that white modern stuff that Charlotte used to listen to now and again on her record-player. You'd think it was all lovely washing over you, then that sound would come and shred your nerves to bits.

As we got into the car for that last ride to Virginia, I looked back at the brownstone that had held me in its grip for the last thirty-five years or so. While Preston bothered the movers about how and where to put what, I could see myself through the kitchen window, the flowers that always announced the spring on our street, no longer there:

I sucked my breath in so hard, I almost lost my balance. My feet were pressed in on that bare kitchen floor. Pressed in and nailed. Fastened.

Unable to move. I rocked and reeled and never left my spot. Daggers dug into my chest. There was no air. I couldn't leave. Ever.

Charlotte came running. Panting. Her little red overalls black at the knees. 'Mommy, Mommy. Please. Come here quick. Look. Look at what I found.'

Her pink palms turned toward the sky; eyes lit up with wonder. Her smile love and trust. A doll. Golden curls. No arms, no legs and black holes in her forehead. I tried to move. So hard I tried. Couldn't. Clamped. I leaned forward slowly and my arms flowed, reaching out. Through slammed doors and silent sulks. Through: 'You can't tell me' and 'Oh yes I can.'

Through music and cut glass and color and dancing and spilled dreams and hand-me-down horrors that this family still can't get straight.

'Oh, my darling, I'm coming. I'm coming to you right now, my sweet. My precious one. Right now.'

Then Preston's voice came at me like hot lead:

'Good God, woman. I've been talking to you for ages. Where have you been? It's time to go. Do you have everything?' I knew that everything I could possibly take with me, I had. The rest seeped through the walls and floors, looked back at me through windows and echoed down hallways. 'Yes, Preston, I have everything; everything I can carry.'

When the car bumped along the old, untarred road, I turned and saw the river. Even Preston's voice couldn't stop me from hearing it, even though I don't think any one really could from the road. But I could. It bubbled and gurgled. And sang. Always sang. But when I looked down as we crossed the bridge, it was just like some giant's brown spittle. Not much left of it now. At least, not around these parts. But I was sure that the mouth was still wide and full. I'd have to go and see once we got settled in.

It took forever. Chopping trees. Laying carpets. In and out of boxes, cases and dry fields full of spite and sand. I tried to get comfortable. I tried to like this place. This place so far away from anything except a dark doe eye and the crawl of a copperhead.

It all came back to me as we moved this, transferred that. I looked out and saw this swampy, miserable place and remembered what I wanted to forget:

A snake. God. I hated them. So scaly and silent. In the yard, Chester had his hatchet. Doing an up and down dance. Toe-jump-heel-jump. That slithering thing. All flat in the front and red-brown, almost the color of the river bank. My brother took a high leap and landed. Chop. A big red burst and that agitated rope finally stayed still. I was so relieved. 'Cause Alexander was coming in about a half an hour and I was already so excited that the armpits of my white linen dress were turning ringed and yellow.

I was fixing the lace around my collar when I heard his voice. My eyes got all blurred and I felt like I had just swallowed a glassful of sand. His warm, brown sound came right in. 'Hello, anybody home?' So tall. So tall and elegant. And well-spoken. Each word like a shiny jewel. He was a teacher in Richmond. I met him at my Uncle Howard's house. Uncle Howard owned a bank, imagine that! A black banker, first one in Richmond. He looked white though. Wanted to adopt me when I was little. Poppa said no, he needed me on the farm. With Momma dead and gone, needed a woman's hand. As many as he could get.

But here was Alexander. In the house. Making it look a bit shabby, even though it was big. Big and long. One room to the next to the next. Then all the bedrooms upstairs. We were sitting talking with teacups on our laps. And cakes I had made. And the world was a perfect, pretty place.

Poppa placed his feet hard against the floor. Each step an assault. Slow and steady. We could hear him coming. Taking a lifetime. Could feel foul filling up the whole house. In he stepped. Striding through, never turning. Speaking all the while: 'Get that nigger out of my house this minute. And don't let him come back.' Never a pause, never a waver. Never. Never. Never again.

I found myself staring out of the screen door that Preston had cursed for hours fixing. It seemed like all the dust and dirt of the world was in my throat, so I just walked away from all that clutter. Boxes within boxes. Into a cool, covered place. Tall pines gathered together to keep that yellow ball from burning me to death. Walked on a soft carpet of brown-green needles. Listening for that sound, those voices. Always heard them when I came down here from New York. The sound led straight to the sand-shelf and then the river water, where I used to put my hot, little feet in when my shoes hurt, which was most of the time. They were always way too small. Had to take whatever you were given. Didn't matter about the size. Just so's you had some shoes on your feet. Had big feet now, swollen from too much standing and bunions from too small shoes.

Slid my toes in. Water a bit of cool, a bit of warm. Sat there moving my legs like scissors. The water churned up and waves pushed their way further onto the grassy sand and up to my waist. Then heads rose straight from that place where the river seemed angriest. Saw Momma, Poppa, all my family that had gone before me, rising up. All coming out of the water to stroke me, to hold me and tell me they were glad I came back. All talking at once: they were lonely, anxious about the land, worried about their river. Too many sick things, rotten things, festering things, they said. Asked me to fix it, look into it, change it. Bring back the big sweep of the tide, the dance of the jumping fish, the drum-beat of the beaver.

The sun was shining on my head and their faces were shining in my eyes. The chorus got louder, their pleading more urgent. My mouth moved so fast you could hear the wind snapping against my lips. My hands were flying over my head, sweeping the sky. Words bunched in my mouth, trying to explain. It was all too complicated, too much, too late. I was up now and running, following them into the water, my voice ringing in my ears.

I bent like a bow as something was being pulled out of my chest and into that river. Down and deep and down, down. Part of me went with them on that burning day and never, ever, ever came back.

IMPRINT

As I walked into the kitchen, Mom's arms were whizzing. She placed plates on the table while simultaneously stirring pots on the stove. I watched her beautiful, broad hands with their long and expressive fingers make a nondescript table into something beautiful. I had felt that hand once: a sharp moment that etched respect for her in me for all time. It had stung so much that my eyes smarted and I'd run to the mirror to see. There it was. Five red prints, each distinct in their intensity, deep and brooding in their anger: a whole hand, on my face. My mother, Estelle, had left her imprint.

I couldn't keep up the work at my prestigious new school. When I left the old one, I'd had prizes and accolades, but no education. Junior High School 22, in Harlem, was into revival shows, musicals. I painted backdrops and breezed through classes where singers, dancers, and actors all gathered together to see our algebra teacher get exasperated each day, only to flick open the *New York Times* and read silently, while black minds invented a world where they thought they needed no education.

What I said to Mom was, 'Why don't you know any French? But I guess you barely know English'. At that shifting moment, I went from a spoiled, self-hating fourteen year old to a self-hating young woman who understood that she understood nothing.

After she'd set fire to my face, Mom stood still, her bearing rigid, phlegmatic. A hundred lost histories swelled in her eyes. Then, turning with small precise steps, she'd propped herself in her chair and covered her face with the print of another day's news of loss and fury.

The mirror in our vestibule, long and rectangular, beckoned again with its icy presence. I went closer, almost kissing it, as I'd tried to see something not yet reflected. What I saw was an oblong, yellowish face, slapped red, with brown eyes full of urgency and disillusionment: a child straining to be something she could not quite become.

I moved away, water glistening on my swollen cheek as I gazed at Mom. The paper was down, the hands clasped tight, only her searching eyes and softly parted mouth let me know that there was still some love left.

Mom leaned her head back. Her lips moved in a silent monologue, as she tapped her toes. She was gone from me now, into her own world of tranquillity.

Estelle:

It was five in the morning and so cold. I put my clothes on underneath the covers, always finding a button missing and searching for a pin. 'Estelle!' Poppa's gruff voice broke up the darkness; as we all clambered about trying to do chores fast enough to walk the two miles to school.

First, it was her lip. It kept creeping closer and closer to her nose. On the right side. As if she were lifting it up so as to pick a particle out of her tooth. I don't remember the whole of her face. I was too young to frame her and keep her clear. But her mouth: Momma's mouth stayed with me and what was eating it stayed with her, as the cancer grew and took her. I was four when she left, and I missed her warm and calming presence. That space never filled: a desire gnawed at me, day after day, year after year.

Our big farm had all manner of animals, and acres of garden to tend to. Nobody was to leave. This was about mouth-feeding. Book-learning was for those people in the other county, where whiteness washed the crackling earth green and prosperous. This is what Poppa thought, his second wife gone, after eleven children, why waste hands?

I was trouble. Always dreaming. Looking through a window, a door, any space that showed a horizon with a future in it. The crumpled newspaper lay waiting for flame. All bunched up against the stove, next to the wood. I wanted it. Took it and smoothed it out along the floor. There in black and white, a chance to escape. My fingers pressed against it, touching a dream. There was such a clear, clean pattern.

Beginnings started with a big letter, only to trail off to smaller ones. Sometimes, in the middle, a letter would stand taller, as if it had to be recognized above and beyond the others. Then the curvy ones would hug close to the stiff. It wasn't particularly pretty, but each letter held a fantastic mystery.

My fingers pressed even harder against each one, in the hope that these words would come through to me and explain themselves. Closing my eyes, I waited. Nothing. I looked down and then saw, where once there was clearness, was now only a grey, smudgy blur. My damp and excited fingers had erased my hopes. I wondered if I became calmer, would these words ever become clear and answer all the questions that pushed my small, but swelling head, to bursting?

It wasn't long before I heard Poppa's voice rip through the frame of the door: 'Estelle. You'd better get that little body of yours in motion out here, or I'll have to get the strap.'

Kicking the words of wonder away, I leapt up to greet the earth that always seemed to stay beneath my fingernails, no matter how many years of washing.

Uncle Howard and Aunt Beatrice wanted it; wanted me, badly. I wanted it too: some special dream of living in a big, white house, with all sparkling and clean things, pretty patterns and new, crisp dresses. Dresses you could almost see through, with some smooth, glidy slip underneath with lace; ribbons of peach and butterscotch. Shoes that fit and a schoolhouse. Everyday. And a place of books when I was not in the schoolhouse: all those green, black and deep red bindings, with gold letters. And black. And white.

They said they wanted to take me there. Adopt me. I was their special one. Uncle Howard said that even though I was the quietest, my eyes reached for a bigger place. He could see the smartness in the pupil. Wouldn't Poppa let me go and live with them? He'd do good by me; plenty of money; bank and all. But no, Poppa said I had to stay and help. So, Uncle Howard and Aunt Beatrice went back to live in their big house, he to run his black bank, she to make cookies for no-one in particular. Poppa must have made some kind of promise though, 'cause, after a while, I could walk those two miles to school at least twice a week. I considered myself lucky. If I counted all the days each year, I figure I'd sat in that little dusty schoolroom about three to four hundred days or so of my entire life. That was real privilege, Poppa said.

Mom shifted in her chair, opened her eyes and looked at her hand — wide, strong and solid. I looked at my face, still smarting. My lips mouthed the words, barely audible, 'I'm sorry. I didn't mean it.' But I did and didn't. Why didn't Mom know more, or at least enough for me? Why didn't I know what all these white kids knew? Why was I running some mad race that kept me out of breath and never the winner? It wasn't fair.

Then, too loud for the room, I said, 'How come we don't know as much as other people. White people, I mean?'

Mom shot a glance through me, almost ripping my head open. With words encased in ice, she said, 'They don't want black people to know anything. Knowledge is power.'

'But you're not black. How come you don't know all this stuff either?'

'Black, Indian, what's the difference? Their dreams of "wipe-out" started long ago, for both of us, and they're still at it.'

Slumped by the wall, with a stinging face, the flash of the reality of who we were, what I was, came home and set my whole head aflame.

'You've got to be better than. You just can't be good. It's not enough. And even then, there's still no telling.'

Mom picked herself up from the chair and the newspaper fell to the floor. The boxes in the word-game jumped from the page. All filled. All finished. All correct.

The pots made their percussive outcry louder than usual. Mom swirled this way and that, the air around her letting me know she had had enough. She could do this, be a presence not really there. I was often reaching out and touching air; ephemeral. Sometimes she was just this great mass of love I could not hold. Silence her shield and her flight. I wondered where she was now: the onions sliced like diaphanous half-moons, the chicken losing its bulk limb by limb, the deft hands making light work and memorable food.

As I watched these silent, intricate manoeuvres, her hands flashed. They danced, they moulded, they held. Held me in spirit and in heart. No need to touch, they were the binding agent; keeping me with her and from the breaking point. Holding and holding up; firm, immutable.

HOT MEAL

'PRESTON, why can't we have them to supper?' Mom said.

'That old hard-jaw, broad-backed heifer never even liked me. And that sad-assed thing she call her husband, well, if you ask me, he's a poor excuse for a man.'

'How can you talk that way about Sadie and Franklin? Remember all those lovely vegetables they used to send to us in New York every summer?'

'Yeah. Half the time the greens would be all wilted and the tomatoes squashed. Who in their right mind would send vegetables through the mail in ninety degree weather? That family just isn't right. I mean, just look at them children, especially the girls. You sure got some crazy relatives.'

'Well, at least there is kindness in their craziness. More than I can say for you.'

'Oh, alright. Go on and have them over. It will be the first and last time, I'm telling you. I don't want that much madness in my house for too long. It might be catching.'

They sat across the table from each other continuing to build the wall they had been constructing for years. After an uneasy minute, Mom got up and started humming as she placed the dishes in the sink. She seemed to be humming an awful lot these days. It wasn't a happy hum, either; more of a drone, on and on, never finding a resting place.

After washing a few dishes with the care and delicacy of bathing an infant, Mom paused from her one-note symphony:

'What would you like for dinner, Charlotte, when Sadie and family come? Do you think Henrietta could come too? It sure would be lovely to have her. She was the sweetest child. And smart, too. I bet no one ever asks her to eat out or anything.'

'Hmm, succotash and anything else you want to go with it. I think the Henrietta idea is super. Maybe Eddie too, but I doubt it. Family gatherings seem to upset him.'

'I don't see why. If everybody just relaxed we would all have such a wonderful time.'

Dad shook his head, his eyes saddened by Mom's optimism. I wondered sometimes if Mom had taken to day-dreaming. Reality slipped away so suddenly, so smoothly from her, leaving just a faint replica of what really was. Her lips always tilted upwards, when she altered her world, and all the frowns from her forehead disappeared. It was a pleasant place she was in, so why should I destroy it?

The cicadas were in glorious harmony, each little group swelling the sounds of the other. The sky tried hard to hold onto its bright yellow glow, but was fast giving way to the lavender-grey wash that draped itself over the horizon. It was seven-thirty, and we heard:

'Henrietta, what in God's name you doin now? Put that plant or whatever it is down and come on. We ain't got all day to be waitin for you.'

Sadie had spoken and announced their arrival.

She was first in, her step hard and forceful. Cousin Sister skittered into the house, almost falling over her feet. Then Henrietta, careful and wary. Franklin came last, bowed with pinched eyes.

'Where's Eddie?' I said.

'Oh, he might be here a little later. Said to start without him.'

I knew then my hope was all I had of Eddie that night. I wished he had come, though. He could ease what looked like a tightly-coiled affair. Plus, he always made everybody laugh. As I began to envision his easy, expansive smile, I spotted Cousin Sister wiggling behind her chair, as if in a dance:

'Food comin?'

'Yes, just a minute,' Mom's voice sang from the kitchen. Sadie shot her a glance that would shatter glass.

The chicken, crisp and golden, took center stage. The supporting cast of succotash, green beans, mashed potatoes, summer squash, biscuits and iced-tea were ringed around it. Cousin Sister sat first, talking as she pulled the chair back from the table, 'Boy, this sure look good, Aunt Estelle. Can I start now?'

A voice, gentle and floating said, 'Why don't we wait until everyone is seated before you start? That would be the nice thing to do.'

'OK, Aunt Estelle, I'll wait, but it sure is hard. I really want to be eatin now.'

Sadie slammed the air with, 'Ain't you got no manners? You act like I ain't taught you nothing in this life. Shut your mouth and wait till we all gets seated. Hummph. You sure is one pain.'

Cousin Sister made a face like she had a really bad taste in her mouth and Henrietta just started laughing:

'ain't nothing change here. people still tryin to beat each other up, when they should be huggin. i know now never to be lookin for no huggin. huggin bring pain. i squeeze the word and the word squeeze me. make me smile. make me twirl. i'm holdin onto the word.'

'Oh Lord, girl. Whatever is you talking about? Always talkin rubbish. The both of you. Just be quiet and eat this here lovely dinner that been made for you. Please, I'm sorry. I don't know what gets into these two.'

'What gets into them is your meanness. If there was some love getting in, they'd be smiling right now, wouldn't you girls?'

Franklin leaned back in his chair and took a deep breath. His chest puffed out and a look of self-approval crossed his face.

Both Henrietta and Cousin Sister put their heads down and stared at the blue and white plates before them. Dad mumbled to whoever might hear him, 'I told you so,' and Mom stood up and held the platter as if showing off a trophy, 'Chicken, anyone?'

Although it was hot, the air grew icy as everybody concentrated on gathering food on their plates, then eating it. Silence stilled the room for a short while, then Sadie said she wanted to 'bring something up' with Preston. Sounding deeply uninterested, Dad said, 'Sure, what is it?'

'Well, I hate to tell you this, Preston, but you been livin on some land that belong to me.'

Dad wrenched back in his chair so hard, I thought he would topple over.

'What the hell you talking about woman? You must be as crazy as the rest of your family.'

Franklin jumped up. 'Who you callin crazy?'

'Oh, sit back down, you fool,' said Sadie. 'You ain't got the sense you was born with.'

Franklin turned towards her, his hand searching for cutlery.

Mom said, 'Now, now, everybody please. We could settle this without all the shouting. I'm sure it's just a little misunderstanding.'

Her gentle voice floated through the room and seemed to settle everyone. Sadie cleared her throat and started in again. 'The people that sold you the land made a mistake. There's about one-sixteenth of an acre that belongs to me, and you growin carrots on it. It starts from the road straight back to the woods. You done planted on that land, so either you gives me your crops and plant where you suppose to, or there's gonna be real trouble here.'

Dad's mouth twitched so hard, his lips had refigured themselves. His fists lay at his sides, knuckles whiter than snow. His chest heaved in jerks and swells and the tanned ruddiness of his handsome face had gone. He was ashen all over, except for his eyes. They were ablaze.

'Get out of my house, you piece of low-life stupidity. How dare you come in here and lie like that.'

'It ain't no lie, Preston, and I got the plat of property to prove it.'

'So do I. I'm gonna get someone up here to settle this whole mess. It's my land, I bought it, paid cash and you ain't gonna take it away from me. I don't care if it's only an inch, it's mine and it's gonna stay mine. You didn't say nothing when I bought it. Why you bringing it up now?'

'I just realised it, when I looked at the papers the other day. It's my land, and I'm gonna get it back, or you're gonna pay me for it.'

Everybody's plates were still half-full, but eating was on nobody's mind, except Cousin Sister's. She had finished two helpings and in the midst of flying words, piped up with:

'Is there any dessert? I know Aunt Estelle can really bake. I wants some dessert.'

Everybody spun around to stare at her:

'Well, I do. I don't care 'bout y'all. Go on and keep fussin. I wants to eat.'

Mom said, 'Yes, dessert sounds like a wonderful idea,' and made her way into the kitchen.

Henrietta started laughing again and then began to sing:

> *we's a family full of hate*
> *ain't no love, can't relate*
> *it's way too late*
> *our kindness is out of date*
> *this be our fate*
>
> *them ol white mens from long ago*
> *would be so happy just to know*
> *they did they work well, we can show*
> *that love is gone and hate do flow*
> *and looks like ever will it be so.*

She was rocking back and forth in her chair, her laughter rising higher as she kept repeating her song, over and over.

Dad said, 'Enough is enough. I think everybody ought to go home now.'

Franklin jumped up: 'You can't be telling us what to do. You can't talk to my family like this. Who you think you is, comin here, telling everybody what to do?'

'Look man, I just think things is pretty bad right now.'

'You sure right they bad, and they gone get worse if you gives me trouble over this here land. Yeah.'

Franklin said all of this, but there was little conviction in his voice. I found myself frozen in the midst of all this anger. Where did it come from? It was breaking my heart. I couldn't begin to think of anything to say to make things better. By this time Henrietta had gotten out of her seat and was dancing around the table, singing her poem. Cousin Sister kept wanting dessert and Franklin sat poised for something, although what it was seemed to baffle him. Sadie and Dad kept batting ultimatums back and forth until Dad thundered, 'All of you, get out of my house now.'

At that moment Mom entered with a lemon-meringue pie. 'Would anybody like dessert?'

THREE

HOME TRUTHS

THE CAMERAMEN had just finished shooting and the glare of the lights hampered my vision. Manhattan seemed hazy and unfocused, as I stepped from my balcony back into the apartment.

Mid-afternoon, with a glass in my hand, I slumped onto my over-stuffed sofa and tried to grasp what had happened. Big time now: two major awards, work exhibited in London and Paris, as well as Washington DC, and LA, living in a duplex on Central Park West. I felt like I was in a dream, but couldn't figure out if it was good or bad.

I remembered when I was near the river, the sand and water running through my hands. I felt the grit, let it rub against my fingertips, then saw all the colors it held in that fierce sunlight. I had it, at last, and ran all the way back to the house like I did when I was a little girl, wanting to shout, 'Mommy, Mommy, look what I found'.

After returning from Tidewater, I was sure all was clarity and light. I plunged into work with such ferocity, that my friends thought I had mutated into someone they hardly knew. Days drifted into nights, nights into weeks, weeks into months. I was so full of ideas I was about to burst: collages, sculpture and now mixed-media. This new work was really different, as each work contained, through its essence, its own history.

Grinding the malachite, I had decided to use my own minerals and plants, as many as I could from Virginia, having brought back a huge bag of sand from the lip of the Tidewater River. Each work held these natural pigments made from azurite, ochre, cinnabar, as well as so many others. Alongside were colors crushed from Virginia creeper, pokeweed berries, rose hips, iris roots and walnut shells, which gave a most intense brown. Sand gave dimension and texture, and the African fabric brightness and geometric complexity. It looked so different, yet so natural. I was ecstatic: all old — all new. So many showings, my work was everywhere. And so was I.

It felt strange, this half-step above most of my friends and acquaintances. I met the old and new major names in my field, all of us sharing the bright patina that glossed over our lives. Glasses raised, we toasted our privileged destinies, most with averted eyes.

I was on my third glass of wine and it was only four-thirty in the afternoon. I had to go to some gathering or other for something or someone that had completely slipped my mind.

'Show up,' my agent had said. 'You don't have to stay long, Charlotte, but at least show up.'

He had to remind me of these events, as they grew increasingly less important to me. Some folks would pull me aside at these gatherings and say things like: 'Why don't you try addressing the white experience in America? Why aren't there any references to whites in your work? Wouldn't it be a more balanced representation? More "now"?'

I often wondered if they questioned white artists in the same manner.

'When I see myself in your people's work, then that will be my green light,' I replied.

'Charlotte Rodgers?' said the man in the severe black suit and shirt.

'Yes, I'm Charlotte Rodgers.'

'I'm Fredrick Masterson, the art critic. I've been following you and your work for some time. It's quite something that a black, especially a black female artist, rather than a singer or an actor, has managed to make such a mark in the world. You must be very proud of yourself?'

'No, not really; just consider myself lucky. Would you excuse me a moment, there's a friend I see that I must catch.'

'Oh, yes, but please come back. Thought we might get together and have dinner sometime. I can tell already it would be a great evening.'

'Yeah,' I said, as I slid away from this thin man with the tight mouth and made my way over to Whitman, stopping on the way to take another glass of champagne from the waiter's tray.

He'd changed so much. The darting, devious, brown eyes now held steady and sure. Whitman was taller and his chest had filled out. He dressed with an artistic flair, African designs on his tie and on the little cap he was wearing. His smile was wide and warm, almost welcoming.

We hugged, slight stiffness keeping us from really touching, as he said, 'Charlotte, you look so fine, girl. And tearing up the art scene, too. Got the whole world in your hands, huh?'

'I wouldn't go so far as to say all that. Just my time now, maybe yours tomorrow.'

Whitman was a writer. He had small successes, but nothing major. His writing was excellent on a cool, detached level. All the characters were always alluding to books read and philosophers pondered, but no one was ever quite believable. He just couldn't seem to get to the core of any truth. And his women characters always had to suffer, as if they were never quite good enough for happiness. Thinking about his latest book brought back that night:

Whitman opened the door, hands shaking and voice trembling: 'Looks like there's nobody here. Jackson must have gone out to get some refreshments with the rest of the gang. Everybody will be back soon, I'm sure.'

I looked around the apartment. Disheveled and dusty, with no furniture moved for dancing, there was no sign of a party.

'Whitman, where are the decorations? It doesn't look like Jackson's done anything.'

'Oh, you know, he's a last-minute man. He'll pull it together. Meanwhile, we might as well make ourselves comfortable. How about a drink? Jackson must have something here.'

As Whitman rummaged, I felt myself sinking. There was a sense of uneasiness clinging to the moment. There were lies all around.

He returned with two glasses of scotch and soda and asked me to sit on the sofa. Firmness entered his sound and with a deeper, more assured voice, he said, 'How about Johnny Mathis? You're crazy about him, right?' I nodded in agreement as the whiny, silken tones softened the tension and filled the gaps of silence. After aborted sentences and wary advances, thin, brown fingers found their way to my face, as Whitman pressed his lips against mine, his mouth chapped and peeling.

As our lips rubbed, there was insistence, a rush that was never there before. As he pressed harder and harder against my mouth, I could feel my teeth cut against the inside. Whitman then threw himself on top of me and hands began to push and probe. Grasping and panting, Whitman struggled to release me from my clothes, while I fought to release myself from his grasp.

The fighting and the grunting went on, until his tongue found mine and a wash of wanting took over all previous thoughts, ideas and feelings. It was as if I had become a woman, although not quite seventeen. I felt stretched, liquid, more than myself. As he was about to enter, I whispered, 'Have you got protection?'

'Of course, baby. Of course.'

I got Roberta to buy it. She looked older and used to get it for her mother. Just a small bottle. The girls in my class told me it would work. I drank and drank, letting the acid burn my insides, as I prayed for an end to this nightmare. Toothpaste and chewing gum were my allies; gin my answer.

No period, not even after sickening bouts of booze, as well as bicycle riding and throwing myself down a short flight of stairs. Where was the blood? That deep red stuff that gave me such pain and that I hated, but now wanted more than ever. Weeks went by, until the call. My best friend was now going out with Whitman. Said it was just a joke. To teach me a lesson. Should never have gone into the apartment alone with him. Nice girls don't do that.

'I'm not pregnant?'

'No. He was wearing a condom.'

'Why didn't he say so?'

'I just told you. He wanted to teach you a lesson.'

I was standing there shaking from the memory, when the champagne passed and I grabbed another one.

'You're going through that stuff pretty fast, aren't you?', Whitman said.

'Just like him', I thought. 'Still a judgmental bastard.' As I stood there for that interminable minute, I realised I really couldn't stand him. If he was the best thing in the room, then it was time to go.

'Whitman, I'd really love to stay and talk, but I don't want to deny you the chance to put some other woman down. Enjoy yourself.'

I rushed out of that room full of preening and pretence and headed for my favourite restaurant, a little Cuban joint on the corner of 82nd Street and Amsterdam, serving the best rice and beans in the world.

Later, full, but wanting, I strolled into the neighbourhood jazz club, where Trevor and I used to go. I always felt at home here, everybody laid back and listening. Trevor tried to really immerse himself in the music, but you could see somewhere between the second measure of the sax solo, and the end of the piece, he was lost, but not in music. He just couldn't get the hang of it. He seemed to hate me for understanding it. I had been listening since I could hear, as the sounds sailed through the rails of my bed and into my little ears. Dad was forever playing somebody: Fletcher Henderson and his band, Count Basie, Ellington, Lester Young, oh everybody. And the singers too: Billie, Sarah, Ella, Betty and Carmen, except he never had anything good to say about them. The singing was terrific, but no decent woman would ever be in a profession like that. He said, 'We all know what they are: just nasty, black whores.'

Sometimes it was really hard to hear the singing, with Dad's voice jarring against their spectacular sounds.

'Why can't they stick to the melody more?' Trevor said.

'Because to improvise, to invent, is the whole purpose of jazz.'

'I know, Charlotte,' said Trevor, almost snapping, 'but they just seem to go too far. I need to hear the melody. They should think more about their audience.'

'They do think about their audience. They just assume that you're free enough to go with them. It's an exploration, an adventure.'

'Well, it's a trip I'd rather not go on.'

I sighed and suggested we get another drink. Blur was better than blatant truth; I fought to be a part of my people and he was in constant battle with them. I had to face the hard certainty of it: I loved Trevor, but I wasn't sure I liked him very much.

Sitting at the checker-clothed table, all these moments leapt up and rattled me. When had I last had a relationship? A real, deep and passionate one? I just couldn't seem to find anyone. Nothing worked with anybody and I kept telling myself it was them, not me, but I wasn't so sure anymore. Plus, work was becoming a real chore now, some sort of theatre experience. It was all lights, camera and smiles, smiles, smiles. Work just didn't enter into the thing. It seemed like all the people in the art world wanted me to act at being an artist, but not really *be* an artist. It was as if the more money I made, the more famous I became, the more they wanted to shut me down, silence me.

The sirens shrieked and the cars honked at each other in ferocious argument, as the musicians fought with New York's constant cacophony. As the night wore on, people sat in the club and began to talk at each other, only a few listening closely to either the music or to what was being said.

I left the club and the next thing I knew, I was cushioned by deep leather seats in a private compartment, listening to the bellowing wail of the train as we left another station. Soon, I realised we were near, as the welcome of the crape myrtle seemed to be everywhere and the laid-back baritone voice announced: Richmond, Virginia, next stop.

HEAD SHOTS

'DAD. It's alright. It's me. Your daughter. Charlotte. Remember? Put the rifle down. Please. Put down that gun.'

I pulled up the blankets, shivering, where he had come and whisked them away, like some wild, agitated ghost. He continued to stand there, gun now pointing out towards the sloping hill that rolled to the road. Eyes of crushed stone, body light and held together as with string. I gently guided this wraith back to his bed, turned off the radio that was playing at four a.m., and then went in the kitchen where I clicked off the other one, playing a different tune on a different station.

I tried to go back to sleep, but all the different tunes and voices banged in my head. It was almost dawn anyway, so I gave up the ghost and went in the kitchen to make some coffee.

There was Dad. When did he get up? He glided through this house like a soft breeze. Standing at the window, he searched the grey-blue glass for some sign. He looked this way and that, and then pulled the string on the Venetian blind so hard, that the slats crashed against the window frame. He spun around. 'Move out of the way. Go to the other wall. They can see you from here. They're always watching me. I never get a moment's rest from them. But I know they're out there, and I'm ready. That's why I keep my gun right over there beside the door. Just wait. I'm gonna get 'em.'

He never heard me coming, full of joy and wonder after my bike ride. I flew in the house because I had seen the most incredible red bird, so puffed-up and bright. It was beautiful. Wanted to know what it was. All smiles and big eyes. But what they saw made flame come out of them. Rage beyond eleven years. A need to obliterate and silence. A man. My father.

His voice was blaring as he picked up the bottle and swigged. It cut

101

against the saccharine sounds of Patti Page singing 'Tennessee Waltz'.

'You ain't shit. You think you something 'cause you look white, but baby, all the white women want me. All the black ones too, for that matter. I am the king. Look at me. Fine as I want to be.'

He rocked back on his heels and the butt of it almost slipped past his shoulders. Then he bolted forward. The barrel was now right against her forehead. Just above the ear. She sat still. Mummified. A hollow sound came from her throat. 'Now, Preston. You don't want to do this. Just put the rifle down, dear. Just put it down.'

'Don't push me. Don't tell me what to do. I'm a man. I make all the decisions 'round here. Understand?'

Daddy now moved his body closer, clicking the cock on the gun. His chest touched Mommy's shoulder. He peered down. 'This is it, bitch. I've had enough of you. I'm going for my freedom now. You can't hold me back. I'm too much for you, baby. Too much. Take your old, fat, flabby body to somebody who can't see no more. I'm going for that white, shining star. The one that's so bright she can see all of me and love every inch of it.'

The hollow sound came again, with a slight tremor in it. 'Please, Preston. Just relax. We'll talk about everything. You can do what you like. I still love you. You know I do.'

A grunt filled his chest and Daddy dropped the rifle. He swerved and looked at me, squinting. Then his eyes turned to slits and his mouth a hard, half-moon. 'Fuck all of you. I'm going to bed. I got to get my rest for my new life. New travels. Ya'll can stay here and rot. I'm going to a whiter, brighter place.'

The earth was dry. Cracked and neglected. I hadn't seen it this bad since Mom and Dad moved down here. Not like those beginning years, or even the drought I'd seen before. Where was the burst of red from tomatoes, the fresh sweet of kale, collards, cantaloupe, corn, beans, squash, peach, pear and ripe watermelon? Gone. Like Dad was gone. Dried up and unrecognizable. Was this it? All his life boasting of bravery, only to have his last moments jammed up against glass, in fear, trying to get some clarity?

He was a small man who couldn't bear his size. Large, robust and a fighting figure: that's how Preston saw himself. But it was in the mouth, not the fist or the brawn, where Daddy had his might. Words washed you away or scalded your skin to leave you blistered and naked. Weapons made of tissue and spit. Of surliness and venom.

Cowardliness clouded him in the end. I saw those late-summer Harlem afternoons of double-dutch, watching my father weaving down our street, the blood on his forehead mixing with the white flic-flac of the jumping rope and turning mine ice-cold.

Hatred a part of so much loving. The film of it always covered what should have shone so brightly. The world had worked its magic and rendered a man of intelligence and principle into a husk of himself. Shriveled up and fearful of who he really was. Haunted.

I was haunted too — by him, by this land. Could it give answers to unspoken words, to lives of wanting and people parted from themselves? What had it seen? What could it tell me? It always seemed to pull me out of myself and into it.

When I walked back through the garden, the dry earth had already started to soak up the droplets. The air cracked and the zig-zag of yellow light let me know it was time to run. When I got to the house, though, it was no use. Slick, cold and shaken, I stepped inside.

Dad was sitting in the kitchen, his laugh a high happiness not heard for a long time. Buster sat opposite him, with eyes full of want and sorrow. He'd yes everything Dad said, then laugh so loud it was embarrassing.

'You's so smart, Mr Rodgers. I just think you's the best person round here. And can do so much. There ain't nothin you cain't do, is there?

'Well, I don't think I can knit you a scarf. Ha, ha.'

I was barely noticed when I entered, except Dad said, 'You dripping water. Better mop up the floor when Buster leaves. Oh yeah, Buster, this is my daughter, Charlotte.' Buster said, 'Nice to meet you', as his voice trailed my movements but his eyes never left my father's face.

Dad leaned forward, his hands clasped in prayer and his face losing at least fifty years. He said, 'Let me tell you about this time this white woman fell in love with me.'

I didn't want to see that glow that Dad got when he told this story, so I went into the next room. Thin walls made the conversation hollow, but audible.

'You was with a white woman? Man, you a brave thing.'

'Well yes, I guess I am. Anyway, she was so crazy about me, she'd come over all the time. Friend of my uncle's. Up in Vermont. We'd visit his place, where I'd go hunting. Man, I had me a beauty of a rifle up there and everything. Sure wish I had that one now.'

He cleared his voice hard, phlegm choking him. 'Anyway, she sure was after me. Estelle was there, but she hardly noticed what was going on. You know Estelle, always in the kitchen doing something. Yeah man, this woman was some hot ticket. She was all over me. Her name was Lorraine. Yes, yes. Sweet Lorraine. Hey Charlotte, you remember that song by Nat King Cole? It was called "Sweet Lorraine," wasn't it? Nah, you don't remember. Before your time.'

I put my head around the corner and placed my hand on the cold steel of the double-barrel leaning against the wall: 'Oh yes, Dad. I remember.'

DRESSING

EVERYTHING had changed since I had been down here last. I'd been back a few times before, but never could stay long because of work, or that was the excuse I gave. The last time was the killer. Estelle and Preston were new, old people. People I no longer knew. People I had to wrench from a dream-like existence into a possible nightmare.

Nobody was in the little green and white house anymore. Dad and Mom were separated from each other now, in homes neither had chosen or wanted to be in. Choices had to be made: hard, ugly choices. I felt a traitor and a saviour all at once. It wasn't a happy feeling.

As I approached this large white house, with scattered chairs in the yard and its wooden façade needing a coat of paint, I heard a high-pitched voice coming from the front window. It sounded like a woman, but then again, like Dad. I wasn't sure who it was, but it certainly commanded attention.

'Oh, you look so good. That suit do something for you like I never seen. Look like it blue, but it got purple in it. And that desk you sittin behind. What that wood be – maple? And so big!'

Then the voice spiralled downwards, with a deep resonance. 'That's what I am, darling. I'm a big man. A forceful man. A man of many possibilities. I've finally become who I am. Watch me swiveling in my chair and looking down on the city. It's all mine, now. Don't have to answer to any damn body anymore, ever.'

Then, the voice boomed and rattled, both at the same time, 'I am a man. The man. You will bow down. Now and always. You hear me?'

The voice then receded and became an echo of itself. 'It was a closed door; deep, dark, with no flame. That's what it was, all my life, fooling people, fooling myself. Peeking out when no one was looking, bending at every corner: the blackness, the bottle, the battle gone to dust.'

When I pushed the screen door open, I could smell it as she screamed, 'Oh, Mr Rodgers! Look what you've gone and done.'

As I climbed each step, the deep mumbling bubbled up. 'Thank you so much. Yes. I know. Isn't it the most magnificent car you've ever seen? I saved and saved for so many years to buy it. Take a picture of me. Please. I want the world to know what a success I really am.'

'Stand up, Mr Rodgers, for God's sake. Lord, this place is a mess.'

The urine stench hit my nostrils and made it hard to swallow. It was always floating in the air here. Its dark, sweet, acrid smell permeated everything. Now, it flowed along the floor, sliding out of the confines of the bathroom, seeking release along the corridor.

There was Dad: dazed, with his mouth upturned and loose. At peace. Sitting on the toilet.

'Miss Rodgers, *please* get out of the way. Can't you see we's got a big problem here? In fact, we be needin to talk. He's the devil, this one. Can't make him do right for nothin.'

She smoothed her short, straightened hair down, but it just reared back up in anger. She bent to mop, then turned, pushing one front tooth forward, then sucking it back in again. Her eyes went tight: 'You his daughter, right? What is wrong with this here man? Evilest thing I ever done seen.'

Yes, I thought. Who is this man, whose face mirrors mine but blurs when I look at it?

'I'm so sorry, ma'am. I just can't believe he's been this much trouble.'

'Trouble? Honey, this ain't the half of it. If you's got a few minutes, after we cleans up this mess, we gonna go in the kitchen and talk a bit. Meanwhile, we gotta get this stuff straight. Here. Get your Daddy in his room and wash him. He got a basin in there. And put some clean pants on him. He got so many, don't know what to do with them anyway.' She humphed, like she wanted to get rid of the excess air in her chest and said, 'No. I know what he do with 'em. Ha. He wet 'em.'

He whipped it back, cold air cutting my skin. Then the slap, the sting. The scarlet whelts. *My screech, a plangent cry. Before this, I was touching freedom. A new feeling, my body warmed with the feel of soft wool against legs, arms, chest. Then the pale yellow hand, with its tufts of wiry, black hair wrenched me from my cocoon of discovery.*

'Estelle. What is this child doing? What are we raising here? Some kind of freak? She's taken off her pajamas. Lying in this crib with nothing on. Why should a child of three be doing this? Oh my God, Estelle. We've got a real problem here.'

Two soft brown eyes ached and longed for direction. They finally rested on the floor, where a faint and faraway voice said, 'Please. Don't hit her anymore.'

As we walked towards the room, Dad looked up at me with a queer light in his eyes; then said, 'My darling Estelle, so lovely to see you. You're looking wonderful, as usual, my dear. It's so nice you dropped by, but darling, let's go now. I know the escape route. I've memorized it. Turn the corner here, then down two flights of stairs, push those heavy EXIT doors open and there it is: our highway to freedom. Let's go, baby. Now.'

He leaned toward my shoulder. His breath hot and sour as it grazed my ear-lobe. A hiss: 'Listen. You understand me, see? You got the picture on this whole situation. We'll be saving one another. You always believed in me. You the best, dealing with it all and everything. Even if it weren't your plan, you stayed right here. You the best. And still smiling. That's my girl, by God. That's my girl.'

His eyes wept with no tears and his smile was filled with large yellow teeth. Then he jerked his hand away, jumped back and his voice rose an octave and shattered the sweltering air: 'Do you like my new shoes? The leather is soft enough, isn't it? I thought that white was the best color. I know it's the best color for me. I've always known that. Clean, sharp and pure. That's me all over, baby. No doubt about it.'

Dad's face now seemed supple within its rigid framework. Soft and muted. A delicate wash. He reached over and took my hand again. The warmest, firmest grasp he had ever given me.

As I listened, my lips buzzed and I wanted to run. Old age was one thing, but this? Where was my voice? I needed to speak, to say something. My teeth were set and I didn't know if I was walking or standing still. Suddenly my head lurched forward and the words hit the air. 'Stop it, Dad. Just stop it. Come into this room and let me change you. Oh God, please, let me change you.'

'Take that thing off. You look like a bull-dyke. Estelle! Have you seen this? They're calling this stuff fashion. What in God's name you want to look like that for anyway? I just don't understand. Harry comes over here and brings the best. I've bought you some of the finest silk dresses, wool suits, coats and I don't know what all. And your mother always buying you those luxurious night-gowns. Satin, lace, everything. Why this? I just don't understand. Sometimes, Charlotte, I swear, you really test my nerves.'

It was plum herringbone check. A pants-suit, double-breasted, from Bloomingdales. I had worked there and been insulted all summer. Saved and got it. The hippest, most elegant thing around. It felt so right. So me. I looked exquisite until his words turned it into something soiled, cheapened. So, into the closet it went. It hung there for most of its life and I dreamed of wearing it most of mine.

'Look here, Miss Rodgers. Is it Miss?'

'No, Ms.'

'Yeah, well nevermind. The point is that we don't know how to deal with your father. He insults everybody. Calling people black niggers and whores and all kinds. Talkin 'bout, "Who wanna fight. I'm ready, you coward bastard." Did he have a real bad life or somethin?'

Bad life? Who knows, I thought. 'He never talked much about his life before he married Mom. It was OK when I was growing up,' I lied. 'He looked happy in his photos.'

'Yeah, well anyway, like I was sayin, what can we do with him? He be stealin women's clothes, drawers and all. Wearin 'em. God almighty. He be sittin in chairs thinkin he be on the toilet. Then be talkin 'bout, "Where's my gun? We gotta go huntin" and all kinds of nonsense, while he be knockin everything over tryin to find the thing. "A man needs his gun," he say. "This is America." What we got here is a real mess, honey. I tell you the truth. A real mess.'

I was folding up fast, but I pushed myself up and surprisingly, a strong, firm voice grabbed her attention:

'Don't worry, Mrs Plowhard, this problem will be solved very, very shortly. I know you've worked far beyond the call of duty, so an extra bit of money will be sent to you for your care and will continue until we've found a new home for my father. I and my family thank you so much for your compassion and concern. You are a very, very fine and generous woman.'

Her face held a scowl, but her eyes and lips softened.

'Alright, Miss Rodgers. Thank you for taking the time to talk.'

She let the screen door slam as I left.

I walked down these streets of weather-beaten porches, canvas swing-seats and window boxes, avenues echoing a life of 'watermelon' and 'ice-man' cries. In my eye, there was my father in his suspenders, brown and white spectators, sharp part in the middle of his slicked-down hair. A bow-tie bright on his neck, a magnificent mahogany-hued woman on his arm, he whispers in her ear: 'Baby, this is gonna be like nothing you ever known before. Believe me. Nothing.' As he took his last gulp of bourbon, the heat of the night swelled him up. You could barely hear the screen door close.

BLOODLINE

AUNT Sadie was peering through her blinds again, as I walked up the stairs to our house. You never saw much of her any more, just two eyes hungry for something — anything. Ever since Dad won the case against the land, she's been like this. As soon as I turned and looked, you could see the slats of the Venetian blinds slap shut like a clam in distress.

The house lay silent, weary from the trials within. No more humming, cleaning, baking, cooking, worrying. No more mending, crying, shrieking, prancing, boasting, laughing and hoping; only a soft sigh of resignation.

I walked around, touching, smelling — lost. I kept hearing Mom's voice, only to turn and feel the slap of the heat. As I rummaged through trinkets, costume jewellery, hairpins, bills, collar stays and cufflinks, trying to reach either of them, I realised that they, and this house, held onto secrets, giving up little. Like, who was this beautiful brown woman, with long black hair cascading down her back, holding onto Dad's arm, whose photo was tucked into an old suit jacket? And Mom's photo of a handsome, ebony-black man, teeth so white and smile so broad, neatly fitted into a silver locket in the back of her bureau drawer? I slid my hand along silk ribbons, linen handkerchiefs, rings, bracelets, combs and empty leather wallets, trying to hold on; trying to understand. As I fumbled and cried at the loss of all our confused love, I began to know that I was never going to really fathom these two — so close and so far away.

I rattled around in the kitchen, handling the pots and pans that Mom used to speak of love; dishes that stayed in my brain and watered my mouth at every memory. My eyes fell across the table where the three of us grappled with candor and delusion, good manners tightening the vice, except when Dad had his fluid release.

I roamed back into the bedroom, opening Mom's closet. I touched the clothes Mom no longer needed now that she was in the nursing home. Her wardrobe was neat and tidy, with subtle colors predominant, except for the occasional bright red or pink that would shout to be noticed. There was one diaphanous, white dress that had the most exquisite lace surrounding the neckline and cuffs. As I slipped it from the hanger, I could hear her telling the story. It was the loveliest dress she had ever had. Uncle Howard had given it to her for her birthday.

I was so happy that day and everybody was just staring at me. I even had white ribbons in my hair and all the necks swung as I entered the third pew and sat down. I was all bundled up in white happiness and settled down for the sermon. While I was sitting there, I felt a wet, warmth on my seat. I moved a little this way and that, to try to avoid it, but it just seemed to get bigger. Didn't know what to do, so I just stayed there until we sang the last hymn and the service was over. When I started to leave, everybody was staring again. Except this time it was with open mouth and saucer-eyes. It was at my dress, but not because it was pretty. I had pulled the back to the front as best I could and there was the red. All over, and now running down my legs. I knew this was death and I was dying. Right there in church. It wasn't private. Everybody knew. Everybody knew but me, that this was the end of little Estelle, getting ready for the blood of a new life. A life of men and seeing red. A life of more of me to come in the shape of someone else. A piece of me walking away. To her own blood and beliefs. As I ran away from that church, the stain of my shame trailing me, I knew that Poppa didn't care and wouldn't tell. Women's things just weren't his concern.

I stood in the hush of the heat and saw a cardinal on the walnut tree. I kicked through the dry, russet earth and ached. Ached for a mother that knew too much and said too little. She, no longer here, but in some small space, with bed and bemusement, wanting herself back as badly as I did:

I want to put my red dress on. Put it on for Preston. He liked it. And get the table ready for the big Christmas day. I'm gonna lay out all that nice silver and the china and the cut glass and cover up the whole table with it. Everything glistening. Baby coming. There she is. Wish she'd eat.

Get your black hand out of my face. Who you? You ain't none of my kin. My kin Red Indian. Not no nappy-headed big face that I don't know trying to feed me. Get out this house. Baby and I getting ready for the special supper. You ain't invited.

'Charlotte, your Momma is so nice. I just loves her. Sometimes she gets agitated, you know, and start talkin a little hateful, but she don't mean it. Most times, she's just as pretty, sittin up in her bed and smilin like a true-life doll. I sure loves her.'

As Mrs Booker, Mom's caretaker spoke, Dad's voice rushed up hard against my head. I could hear him telling it to me again, with teeth clenched and a voice too loud.

After so many years, it really got to be bad. Then the yelling came. And the screaming. And the meanness. Never. Never was my Estelle like this before. Always calm. Always nice. Always understanding. What in God's name?

The pills were all under the bed. Bottles and bottles. Full of dust. She came in screaming:

'I saw you with that bitch. That young, fat bitch. In the garden, near the shed. You old, bony bastard. Touching her in our garden. Right in my face pressed on the window.'

The knife swung in an arc. Flew past my ear with a wind-sound. 'Estelle, please.'

'Don't tell me. All those years. Waiting. You coming home drunk, night after night. I saw all that lipstick, semen. Listened to all those lies. They'll find out about you, you two-faced son-of-a-bitch. The world will know. And I'll be so glad. Then I can rest.'

112

Her arm went limp and the knife dropped. She looked like a startled deer shocked by the lights of a car. I took her hand. Mine shook like I had palsy. She glanced at my hand in hers. Her mouth opened wider than ever seemed possible. She said 'God' — but it was the voice of somebody not on this earth.

The doctors said they couldn't do the eye operation because she was having a small stroke. They would do another operation, which they said would stop her from having a bigger one. They were going to take her in right then. I don't trust these damn white doctors. All they want to do is take your money and use you for some experiment or something. They don't care if you live or die. I know how they did experiments on black men with syphilis and all. And all kinds of other tricks with Negroes. But the family says, don't worry. It's OK. They'll take good care of her. I went along with the program, but I wasn't happy about it.

I knew it. I just knew it. How could they do this to my Estelle? Like she was a criminal in jail. Flat against the white sheets, her small, babyish head sunk into the pillow. Eyes wide with wonder. Mmmming to herself. God, those straps came from the top of the bed-post and in a line straight to her wrists. Wrapped so tight you wouldn't believe it. Red showing from where they wound the thing. Flesh pushing up. Around and around and around. Then tied to the side of the bed. Legs too. Shackled. Like some prisoner. Some animal. Some slave.

They said something about 'She was walking out of the hospital. Have to keep her in bed for safety reasons. Will hurt herself. Get lost. The operation takes place tomorrow. She'll be home soon.'

Seem like I was drowning in this white sea. White walls, beds, doctors, nurses. They couldn't do this. I was the boss. I made the decisions. They just couldn't do this to my wife. Quietly, looking like I was bending over to kiss her, I freed her. Both arms, then legs. Watching my back all the time, I took her belongings and shoved them in the bag. Then I waited. Waited until it got kinda late and the nurses changed their shift. Lifted her. Put her coat around her small shoulders and placed her feet in her slippers. The exit was real close by. We slipped out. Shivering, I steadied her in the car. Soon *we were home, where she never should have left. I could take care. And then, when she was better, she'd cook me one of those fabulous breakfasts she used to make. She loved doing that. Just loved it.*

I shook myself back to Mrs Booker's puzzled face. She seemed weary and her lips twisted in a failed effort to seem happy. Mrs Booker only had four to take care of, but Mom was further on than the rest. She no longer walked, just sat in her bed and stared. But when I visited, her stare would sparkle. And there was a sweeping smile. And the laughter. And the nonsense language that caused the laughter. Did she know me? Yes, maybe. Then again, as I closed the door on this serene, immobile woman, I knew for sure that she never really knew me at all.

Estelle:

Here comes Charlotte again. Mommy's sweetest thing. She's gained some weight now and looks so much better. I keep trying to tell her this, but she just smiles so hard, with those deep, sad eyes and laugh, even though I know she's breaking up inside.

I got all these thoughts and things, but I know something done gone wrong. Every time I think the words, they don't seem to come out right. Sometimes it just nothing but jumble.

Don't like this place I'm in. Why am I here with all these strange folks creeping around and talking to me like I'm a baby? Every time I get my ideas going and start to tell folks what's on my mind, they just laugh or say something dumb like, 'Oh, ain't she sumpin to look at, all nice in her bed. And still pretty, after all this time.'

Why don't these people hear me? I keep trying to tell Charlotte that I love her, no matter what she's doing or who she's with or what she like or what … my apple pie. Want some now. Love to see them apples. Red, with the little green bits and the sun coming in and making them glow. But I got to get that knife and take away all that cherry color and make that pie.

Preston love that pie. Oh my, my. Look at the window. Here it comes. The big march. Coming in to say hello. All my brothers and sisters, even

Momma and Poppa. They done walked right through the glass, saying they ain't hurt, but I can see they bleeding even though they be laughing and carrying on. 'Cept Poppa. He just stand there with his mouth shut — don't know what he be saying or thinking. He was always like that. Like me too, I float away from everywhere. When I get the cut and blood be running all through my brain and I want to smash the glass, hit Preston, shake Charlotte. I cut off. Not good. Sometimes should talk. Do. When I can. Especially my baby. Need talking. I did all. Gave heart, head, hands. Baby know it. Love always. Love and love and love and bididely-be. Da-doom and whoa yes. Fuzz is everywhere. Being lifted now. Lots of water. Sleeping soon on rose-petals. Deep, dark ones. Cool. So much perfume smell.

Did Baby say something? Who talking? 'I love you, Mommy.' Yes. The love is the all thing. Be peace and water now. Float world. Float.

'You know, your Momma doin pretty good. We's so glad to have you here. She's droppin down a bit, but I guess you done seen that. I just want you to rest assured she's in good hands. You can see that too, can't you? I gives her extra-special care, 'cause she's one good lady.' Her voice was a sigh.

I gave Mrs Booker the pink gown for Mom and pressed my lips against her cheek. The brown rose up with the red and she tugged hard at the drops forming in her eyes.

The old dirt road threw up dust and Cousin Sister was flying through it.

'How your Momma – I hear she doin alright – You think so – How she be talkin to you – Ya'll understand each other – My Momma don't understand me – Shoot, she ain't never understood nobody – But I think your Momma understand – Yeah, I bet she do.'

I wasn't really listening as Cousin Sister flashed through her thoughts. I was letting Mom settle inside me, quiet and strong, and making sure there was always that space and place for her to be. We stopped by the side of the road because Cousin Sister said she had just bought some real sparkling jewelry she wanted me to see. Said she had it in the back of the car.

While she rummaged, I got out and started walking. Smack up against us, along the river-bank, vibrant in the afternoon sun, scarlet, intense flowers. Had never seen them before and bent to their lustre. Picked one and stroked each petal as if trying to extract something from it.

Cousin Sister poked her head around the car and said: 'What you got?'

'A flower.'

'Lemme see it. Oh, yeah. That's the cardinal flower. They say it done been here since our peoples first done come round here, and you know that be a long, long time ago. American Indian thing. I mean, flower. Pretty ain't it? And so bright red. Red as it want to be. Just like a burst of sun at the end of the day. Sort of like life almost, I think. Just keep growin and goin on like that no matter what.'

'Yes,' I said, as I pressed it against my lips hard and felt its softness. 'Yes, it's just like life.'

WHITE LIGHT

THE INDIAN Baptist church stood slightly back from the road, imposing and well-cared for. It wasn't that large, but there was a new paint job and with its white steeple, that reached for the heavens and gleamed in the sun, it stood as a dubious beacon to all Tidewater.

I walked between gravestones, some dating back to the late eighteenth century, careful not to step on anything or anybody. A chill came over me, despite the heat, as I tried to keep it together amongst all these spirits vying for my attention.

Our name was on just about every grave. I saw the headstone of a great uncle I had heard about — Zachariah Ransome, who had three wives, because each gave birth to so many babies for him, they just couldn't hold out. I think they said he had twenty-eight children in all.

Then there was an aunt, three generations removed, Wilhelmina, who had become the first Native American teacher to teach at the 'Little Indian Schoolhouse', which used to sit way back from the church, near the river, that only had white teachers before.

All of Mom's relatives were, or would be buried here, except her. There would be no gravestone that said, 'Estelle Ransome Rodgers' in this graveyard. That was because Mom refused to be buried with, or attend the church of, tribespeople who said her mother wasn't pure. Georgina Ransome's hair wasn't straight enough, and whenever she went about town, everybody hissed and muttered. Mom remembered her frail mother crumbling under all the prattle, the meanness:

Poppa's friends huddled a year after the marital ceremony.

'She can't pass the comb test. I'm tellin you man. It's the God's honest truth.'

'But you know how he is about Indian and black and all. Can't be true.'

117

'Yes it is. They say her hair come all the way past her waist, but when they put that comb in it, it never got any further than just about where the middle of her ear was. And his father the Chief and all. Sure must be some kind of embarrassment for him, marryin her. Hope the children come out with real good hair, so's there won't be too much talk about it.'

Mom said that Grandpa was full of fury. He cursed all the folks, saying, 'What do you know about anything? I would never marry no colored woman no how. I don't know why you all carry on like this. Why don't you just go and find some work to do, instead of meddling in other people's business?'

Grandma's hair was just a bit bushy and fly-a-way, yet there was no black person in the family, that anyone knew of. Her brother, Howard Bradshaw, felt since he'd been tagged as one, he had just better go along with the program. Made a name for himself, too — first black banker in Virginia. Who knew what anybody was? All they knew about the family was that they were more white than anything else, if not completely. It seems they came from England, somewhere in the North, and settled in Virginia in the seventeenth century. As indentured servants, they were soon freed and given a bit of land. After that, they began to make strides and prospered.

Mom learned about all of this and made her decision. She never set foot in the Indian Baptist Church, after she got out from under her Poppa's thumb and became a grown woman. The whole Ransome family was deeply saddened by it. They felt bereft at not having their loveliest sitting in the first pew.

I wanted to go in, to see what it was like, but stopped about halfway there. A strong hand was gently pressing down on my shoulder. The voice, my Mom's, was compelling: 'Charlotte, don't go. They made a mockery of your Grandma. You can't let them know you approve.'

'Alright, Mom, it's OK,' I soothed, as I turned to take her hand. But my mother was nowhere in sight — just a hot wind howling.

'Hey girl, what you doin standin in this broilin sun? You ain't got no sense. Wanna go with me? I'm goin to get some barbecue. This place got the best in Virginia, just a few miles from here. Got real good lemonade, too. Pink, if you want. I just loves their lemonade. Come on, girl, let's go.'

Cousin Sister was talking faster than the mosquito buzz circling my head, while the exhaust from the car stank up the sky and the noise from the engine shut up a robin's song.

I looked around again, hesitant, still not quite believing that Mom wasn't there, and finally decided I might as well tag along. Hopping in the car, those old, fuzzy shag seats burnt up my behind. I shook my head at my stupidity. I was going to hate this ride.

Cousin Sister swerved this way and that, sometimes even coming off the road.

'Wanna go with me to this new jewelry store that just opened downtown, when we finishes our barbecue?'

'How come you're so crazy about jewelry? You seem to be more in love with the stuff now, than ever before.'

Cousin Sister cleared her throat and turned the wheel so hard we skidded into the parking lot, barely missing two cars.

'I'll tell you, but I gots to eat first. I'm hungry. Ain't you?'

Without waiting for my answer, she jumped out of the car and rushed towards Bar-B-Q Jack's.

She ordered enough food for ten, then turned to me and said,

'What you want? I'm payin. You can have anything, or everything. Hungh, hungh.'

It sounded like a laugh, yet a grunt, with a great deal of pain mixed in as well. I ordered, then we took our food and sat by the river, at a little picnic table, one of three. There were row boats, sun-scorched red and blue, bobbing on the shore-line and that familiar smell of salt rushing to my nose.

'So tell me, Cousin Sister, you promised. Jewelry, remember?'

'I always loved the sparkle, you know that. I just seems to love it more now. Especially them diamonds, or anything that almost look like 'em. You got any? Lord, I'm crazy 'bout them things.'

119

'Yes, I've got some earrings. That's all. Don't really care, remember?'

'Oh yeah, you said. Well, I got my first and only real diamond when he give it to me.'

'He? Who?'

'Didn't your Momma tell you?'

'You know, my mother was a very quiet woman. Sometimes, too quiet.'

'Well, his name Redmond. He was pretty. No, I ain't kiddin, he was, just like a girl. He had this brown, curly hair; big curls, just bouncin all over his head. And his skin the same brown as his hair. All blend together in one beautiful package.'

'Anyway, he not only the nicest thing you want to lay your eyes on; he sing. I mean sing so as to quiet everybody, everywhere. You just stop where you is when his voice ring out. A sound from where the Lord live, that's what it was.'

'I met him in church, not the Indian one, but the new one up yonder from it. Where mostly black peoples go. I like to mix it up; travel from church to church, listen to the different preachers, see how the womens dress and see they jewelry. I learns something new at each stop.'

'Anyway, he started singing and it seem like that voice just reach inside my chest and found my heart. Grabbed it and held on tight. He looked at me and it was like some laser-beam had hit and run straight through me. That was it.'

'He bought me this sparkling thing and put it on my finger. The ring shine so much, that its sparks fly out and bounce all over the room. He said something real funny when he put it on my finger, though. Somethin 'bout, "That will keep 'em quiet." "Keep who quiet?", I asked, but he just hugged me and said, "Don't worry, little Sister, we makes a pretty picture."

'We got married a few months after that. He used to sing to me all the time, but after we got hitched, he just shut up. Not just singin; talkin too. Seem like I had bad breath or something, 'cause he never came near me. When we gets in the bed, he so far off to his side, it always look like he was gonna fall on the floor. I ain't never had no, you know what, neither. Never.'

'One day, I come home from work early, 'cause my period be botherin me so bad, my stomach just screamin. So's, I go to the drugstore and gets something to kill the pain and heads on home.'

'When I opened the door, I hear all this achy sound and sound like held-back screamin. I move closer, then it sound like people be rushin and whisperin. It come straight from the bedroom. I push open the door and there they was. Just like with Momma and Mr Green, only difference was, this person look just like my Redmond, except for the face.'

'He left after that and ran away with that person in our bedroom. He slipped the ring off my finger while we was sort of fightin and he was grabbin my hand. Yeah, he took that ring with him, and I don't know, ever since then, I been crazy about jewelry. It just make me so happy; it seem like it happy itself, gleamin and twinklin and all. I just wants it, all the time. Somethin happen and the want take over me real, real bad. It whisper in my ear and make me follow it. Push me into places; make me do all sorts of things.'

Cousin Sister's shoulders dropped and she looked down at her feet. I was speechless. I didn't know where to go from here. She looked so helpless, broken. All of a sudden, she reared her head, her eyes beaming brightness and said, 'You hungry? Lord, I sure am. I could eat up everything.'

WIND SONG

TRUDGING under a malicious sun that seemed intent on destruction, my mind trailed back to the last days Mom was at home.

There she sat on the sofa, in her pink, two-piece leisure suit, her hair combed up in a tiny ponytail, with only a few wisps of thin, baby hair. A bemused smile across her face, she lovingly embraced anybody — everybody, although it was clear she recognized no one.

The doorbell rang each morning and Tina, the home-help nurse, stood brightly at the door. She had such blond hair, it almost seemed white. Her long, skinny legs held a thin frame, with bony wrists and long fingers with pink, painted nails. She rushed in, breathed excitedly:

'Hi, how's your Momma today? I sure love to come to this place. It's such a pretty house and your Momma's so pretty too. I think she looks just like Katherine Hepburn, especially with her hair up like that. That's why I brush it up that way. Don't you think so?'

I turned and looked at my mother. No matter how I strained and altered my vision, Katherine came nowhere into sight. I saw a once-beautiful older woman. But Hepburn?

'Maybe you don't think so, but she sure resemble her to me.'

Tina went over and greeted Mom. Mom looked through her and smiled the brightest smile. Tina opened her arms and my mother jumped up and reciprocated. There they were, locked in an embrace, one exuding questionable love, the other – none whatsoever.

'Did I tell you, Miss Charlotte, that I knows that you and me and your Momma is all related?'

I thought, 'Why does she always call me, Miss Charlotte. This isn't Gone with the Wind, and anyway, it makes me so uncomfortable. I keep telling her, just call me Charlotte. Maybe she sees my discomfort and gets a kick out of it. Maybe it's her way of showing respect. Who's to know?

'Oh, really? Where'd you get that information from?'

'I been doing research. A family tree kind of thing and your Momma is definitely my cousin. On her Momma's side. Her Momma was white, or almost, I heard. Anyway, I told my Momma. Lord, I was so excited 'cause I sure do love Miss Estelle. My Momma turn red as a bandana. "Is you crazy?" my Momma said. "We ain't related to no niggers or injuns. I ain't gonna listen to this shit."'

'Please excuse them words, Miss Charlotte, I just was repeating what my Momma said. I would never talk about people like that, especially this here lovely family. I just wanted to tell the story like it happened. Anyway, next time you come down here, I knows I'll have a paper to show you, that will prove that we all kin. Won't that be something?'

I tried to smile, but I don't think anybody would have taken me for a happy, excited person.

'Yes,' I said, sighing, 'It will be something indeed.'

Despite the heat, I decided to take a walk to see Henrietta, as staying home now seemed almost impossible. I had just come from seeing Mom and Dad, each in their separate homes, and felt wrung out, this hateful weather not helping. They were both old now and waiting for a sky brighter than the one above me. Dad just as muddled as Mom, but always putting on his studied charm.

I felt lost. Alone and frightened, in a new world where my confusion and anger had no love to bounce against. I didn't know if I could tough it out for very long with Henrietta, and wondered if I was wise to go and see her, though something in her always helped to make things clearer.

There she was, seated on the porch of Dr Simpson's, with a book grasped in her hand, *From Slavery to Freedom* by John Hope Franklin. She seemed radiant and settled, somehow. Her hair looked lovely and smooth, and her clothes considered before she put them on. She seemed less fidgety and clearer in her eyes. Her face was a vision of calm. Just as I was taking in this new person in front of me, a car sped past us, making Henrietta jump up with a jerk. She pushed me aside and craned her neck so hard, it looked twice its length.

Henrietta:

where that big, sheeny car be goin so fast? make two big walls of dust, just zoomin through here. it were like some silver arrow — just be gleamin. sendin flash up in the sky. pierce the sun and it splinter. air be full of diamonds.

you like diamonds? i ain't never had no truck with 'em, but my sister into that kind of thing. she be buyin these rings and bracelets, with those cut-up colored stones and like to bunch them altogether some time. yes. put them on top of one another. make a big mound. big heap of sparkle. i likes my sparkle to come from my mind, though. out my head.

it just hit me. it be trev in that car. he home. ugh. know he mr somethin. he might be cousin, but he mr nothin to me. he might take up the big screen, but he just a little brown speck the way i see it.

anyway, i ain't got time for no tv or movies. i'm bound to the book. what a world be found in these things. they be tellin me stuff that blow my head through the air. like how when some tired-ass man named polk be president, he and some other white mens want to take over the south of america, then south america and all them tiny little islands be inbetween (charlotte, you remember you brought me a globe? i spin like mad.) these some greedy mens. but we already knows that.

then the civil war. right round here too. some man who name sound like clickin teeth — oh yeah — mc clellan. he be the big one up front, leadin the soldiers. come through here, supposed to be fightin for slaves freedom and he hate niggers. that's what he say. he say he ain't fightin for no niggers, he fightin for a union. who wanna hook up with him? i surely don't know.

while they be fightin and black soldiers be fightin (again), there be slaves done run free. but some havin trouble, 'cause ain't nowhere to go, 'cept maybe to the blue army. through all them zippin bullets and long knives, some black folks be makin it north, where some slap you down and send you back and others just say, OK — you ain't my friend, but i give you some soup and shelter.

i bet be one or two who had fun gettin back at they masters though. jump in closets and come out in stripes and dots. red and green and gold and shinin shoes. oh my! lookin like master with black face and big smile. slidin on saddles attached to trottin horses, buggies, and all kinds of get-away goods. maybe it don't last long, but a bustin-out laugh bounce from field to field before all the fun finish.

it be a bloody mess, though. i seen pictures. lord. blood be everywhere. the indians tryin to keep out of everythin. they real upset 'cause the law words of virginia say they ain't no more. they gone. now they colored. that was some trick back a few years so they be slaves. but they never be. and anyhow, who the law to say who you be? you is you. plus, when somebody call you, you won't know to answer.

i done had me a vision and i knows who i be. ain't no name make no difference. i done found me my inner circle. like a corn-stalk. some deep-planted thing that all me come out from. instead of sparkle, i got nice, soft yellow and brown. autumn end-of-day glow. a calmin color. i been through the back part of my life and although it give me tremble, i'm beginnin to get my mind in a steadier place about it.

besides. i keep hearin that wind-song comin from the river. it be singin my name with a voice of beckon. it say come. come. and i sing back, i'm comin, sweet, sweet salt water risin, i'm comin.

Visitation

A HOT pomegranate stain filled the skies, as the grey-blue receded and gave way to the announcement that tomorrow, the heat was on again. I grabbed a chair from the porch and for no reason that I could explain, took it onto the grass and close to the road. I sat and sat, smelling the pine trees and watching all the little creatures scurrying. They looked as if they had purpose and direction; especially all those shiny little red and black ants, which beat themselves breathless, following orders of an unseen leader. I, in contrast, sat with a mind pitching back and forth, without a clear way forward. It was because the world I knew, or thought I knew, was about to disappear. Mom and Dad were going, or in many ways, had gone. Aunt Sadie was lost to me and her children lost to themselves, at least one of them. Poor Cousin Sister, alone and forever searching for some dazzle in her life, to fill that screaming chasm in her heart. And Henrietta; I saw hope blossoming in her eyes. Could it last?

Two cars were tearing up the road, moving in opposite directions. I sat up, as I saw Trevor coming toward me on my side, and Eddie flying by on the other. Bits of gravel hit my face as I leaned into the road. I waved and hollered, 'Hey, Trevor,' but he didn't see me or hear me. He seemed to be having a conversation, but there was no one else in the car that I could see.

Trevor:

It was ridiculous. What a name. Dwayne. Dwayne Dillon. Hell. Whoever heard of such a name? Well, in fact, most of America had. Let's face it though. It was a simple solution. You know what I mean. That good old leveling process of America. Be like everybody, but nobody in particular. Maybe you could get away with being *you* in places like New York or LA, but for the bulk of the country it was: wear the same clothes, live in the same houses, drink the same drinks, and most important of all, think the same thoughts. Well hell, it got me somewhere. So this is the new me. The old me was Robert Trevor Wilson Randolph Bainbridge, Jr. My parents loved to let it glide off their tongue — the long, resonant roll of it.

'Distinguished,' they said. 'Sound like he should be President or something.'

Yeah, their son the lawyer, doctor, mayor, governor. Grey pin-striped wonder.

'And you got to admit he look so good. I mean, with that black hair that shine like patent-leather, so thick with waves and all. And skin look like straw in the sun.'

Yeah, I thought, running my hands through my soft, sleek strands. Yeah. Momma was right.

My name. Manager thought it sounded too East-coast. Too uppity.

'We need an across-the-board name. An everybody-can-relate-to-it name. An easy, comfortable, everybody-nobody type of name.'

So, I took it. Hollywood took it. America took it. The cameras rolled on and the money rolled in. I was famous.

I pushed the window button in my car, just to get some fresh air. The heat was merciless, but I felt this urge to smell the pines. The stench strangled me. As quickly as I could, I shut it. My God. How could they? How could the county allow itself to get saddled with this? A landfill for other people's garbage! These people were so stupid. Brain-damaged. I felt sour come up into my mouth. No protest, no nothing. Just let the company go ahead and do what they pleased. Well, it serves them right. If they're not going to stand up against this kind of thing, they're just a bunch of lazy-assed …

Now here I am thinking about stuff and this car just whizzed by me and almost took the mirror off the left side of my Mercedes. Damn. Custom-built and all. Just bought this two months ago. Flying. Burning up the road. Yeah, that was Eddie. Give me that scissor-smile of his. We used to be tight. Thick. Home-boys. The best of friends. We were cousins and did everything together, except mess with each other's girls. The cat was brilliant. His brain was so sharp it could sting you. Then one day he just seemed to say, 'Fuck it'. Don't know what happened, but it seemed to be around the time that he and I came to our final blows.

In class. We were all sitting there with pants too short and maybe just a little too tight. Breathing in dust, sand and sweat. The heat in the air was blue-purple and came in waves like the river. My teeth sawed back and forth trying to stay interested in the white drone that drilled through my head and left it empty. Talking about the nineteenth century. America. Mr Forrester, on and on. Suddenly, he got really excited. Agitated, flushed and fanatical. His voice rose and pushed the chalk-dust screen around the room. I leaned forward. Knew this was an important moment.

> *The child-like needs of the slaves …Their inability to cope*
> *with responsibility …Their innate stupidity …A hereditary*
> *thing …Happiest with jobs that didn't tax mental agility …*

Somehow, I started getting very excited too, although I really wasn't sure why. My legs got rigid, knees seemed to lock. Teeth set hard against each other now, a barrier from which I thought nothing could ever emerge again.

Eddie flew up in the air. Beautiful black-red arrow heading straight for the teacher. Arms reaching out like assegai, screaming, 'You sick, racist mothafucka. I'm not gonna listen to this shit anymore. Get outta here before I kill you.'

He turned. Eyes burning at me. 'Come on, brother. Say something. Help me.'

I just sat there. Muscles frozen. Eyes bugged. Smiling, it seems. Smile kept getting bigger, wider. Felt like it took up the whole room. Engulfed everybody. Then this voice, 'Yes. Yes. I know what you mean. Some of our people can be like that. But not all of us. Not all of us.'

Eddie spun. Lunged. Spitting. Screaming. Broke my nose and left a slight scar above my right eyebrow. Held my throat so hard I swear it changed my voice for the rest of my life. Now, it always seems to have a small, hesitating choke in it. Could never tell if it sounded as if I was searching for the exact words, or if I was never quite sure of anything I said.

I needed some music. Something to take me out of myself. My teeth chattered. Maybe the air was too cold. I turned on the radio:

> *Baby, just let me put it there.*
> *Because we just don't care,*
> *How many juices wet my bone,*
> *How many cries fill up the air.*
>
> *So, come on baby, back up to it.*
> *Just let your sweet man put you through it.*
> *Sure thing, ain't nothin to it,*
> *Just do it.*

This slick, buttery voice was slurring its way through a grunt-bang rhythm that was making my head throb. Why we want to sing stuff like that? It's just what these white folks expect us to do. Talk about our women like they're trash. Calling them 'ho's' and shit. No wonder we keep pedaling in the same place.

> *The time is now nine-thirty-five and I'm back with you all to discuss a matter very close to our hearts. Listeners, we need to think about all this violence. We have to protect ourselves, our homes, our children from these people. You know the ones I'm talking about. These gangs. These black gangs. Destroying all that is good and great in America. Arm yourselves, my friends. Get your guns and shoot. It is the only …*

129

The Lord is the true and only way. America is a lost nation, its soul sold to the devil. Put your mind on Jesus …

This is your main man, Jack Sprat, who can eat some fat, as well as lean. So just sit back and dig the smooth, sweet sounds of Smokey singing 'The Tracks of My Tears' …

Tears. They fell and fell and filled up the whole room. Or that's the way it seemed. God. If anybody had seen me then, they wouldn't have believed it. My eyes like the flesh of a raw sirloin. I had never cried so much in my life. The trouble with it all was I didn't know why I was crying. Voices would whirl around in my head. Loud voices. Warm, purring voices. Voices of thunder. It happens down here. This dusty, old dry land that ripped your insides out. That screamed at you and flew up in your face, making you trip on yourself and fall flat. Flat against your 'please let me hide this from the world.' Always asking something of you. A shadow never far behind. A hissing. A whisper. A wail.

That river water. Went in, running. Stung by salt-splash and hot rays. Kept going out, then left, following some pull. Down I went, slow and strong. A mud pull, mud squeeze. Oh Jesus, the swamp. Gulping. Legs like two hundred year old tree stumps. River water stench. In my face, mud, and on my hands. A deep pull from down to up inside, my body lifted and I ran. Ran out of that river, out of that county and far, far away from myself.

I guess I was luckier than Eddie. After that slight altercation, my parents managed to get me into one of those integrated schools in the next county. It was far richer than Tidewater and the level of teaching, books and general atmosphere was far superior to that nebulous business they called school back home.

It had been mixed for quite a few years by the time I entered, so I suppose I felt pretty much at ease. The white girls smiled too hard and the white boys played too rough, but I got through it without too many 'Hey nigger, go on home' or, 'Better watch your back, baboon, 'cause if you put your black dick anywhere near these pretty, sweet white angels of ours, we'll cut it off at the balls. Y'all know we been doin that for years.'

There were a few brothers and sisters there either talking a little too fast or walking with taut, stretched necks as if they were above any worldly concerns. One sister in particular. Walnut with wilful lime-green eyes. A knockout. Married now with three kids. Don't see her much, but I give her all the things she wants and needs. Yeah. My wife, of course. But I'm not the only one in my family making it. There are lots of us holding down good jobs and prestigious positions. Maybe some of us had to swallow a little more shit from whitey than we had anticipated, and put racial issues on the back burner, but we've been compensated ten-fold. You see, through all of it, I've still got my pride. I have absolutely no trouble with how I've conducted my life.

Look. We've made the grade. Done the trip. Cossetted and cushioned in our well-oiled worlds. We're alright and I'm fine. This car purrs like a cougar. My Armani linen suit wrinkles in all the right places. My Italian shoes are so soft it's like walking on smooth, white sand. Everything, we have everything. But what I can't figure out is why this river keeps surging through my brain, throttling my veins and flooding my world. Why it still makes me want to howl, to escape and run to a place where I can, at last have sweet, sweet freedom from myself.

REPARATION

NIGHTS were beginning to get difficult in this house of memories. I rattled from one room to the next, expecting to see Dad from the kitchen window, out in his tool shed, or in the house, mending something or the other, with Mom asleep over the crossword in the living room, television blaring. I paced and became more and more uncomfortable, so I called Darlene and asked if she would like to come over for a drink and something to eat. It had been a while since I'd seen her, as she was away at some Mid-western university doing research the last time I came down.

'Sure, that would be great. Want me to bring anything?'

'No, girl, just bring yourself.'

Darlene got out of her car and started towards the door. She seemed taller somehow, or maybe she was just standing straighter. Dressed in a conservative navy suit, white cotton top and navy sling-back heels, black hair hanging straight down her back to her waist, she looked the business with a twist. Rebellion seeped out, no matter how hard she tried.

Her face was clouded with seriousness as she stepped out of the car, but she beamed when she saw me standing at the door.

'Girl, you look wonderful.'

'So do you, Charlotte. Have you lost weight or something?'

'Just worry. Worry does it every time. Well, come on in. What can I offer you? I've got beer, white wine, vodka and lots of fruit juice.'

'I'll have any kind of juice you've got. Just remember to put some vodka in it.'

Her laugh loosened up, welling as it did from the depths of her stomach to a bright sound, full of music. Facing Darlene across the little

Formica table in the kitchen, as we both picked up clammy glasses filled with ice, I began to tell her about my little triumphs and large dilemmas. She listened, shaking her head and saying, 'Yeah, girl, I know what you mean' and 'But look what you've already done.' We went on that way for quite awhile, until I noticed that Darlene wasn't too forthcoming with her own stories. I told her to 'drink up' and made sure that our next drink packed a real punch. She took off her jacket after a bit and seemed to relax, but it was when I mentioned Trevor that she came to life.

Darlene:

I hear he's back. Certainly not for long, though. My cousin never did stay long. In and out like a hurricane. Stir things up, topple things over. But we always put them right again after he leaves. Every female smitten, swooning, stammering and full of light-eyed wonder. Even me. He had us all pressing for a look, with those jet eyes that would turn your chest to stone and your stomach to syrup. Smooth, supercilious and bad as he wanted to be. Women are still falling, but I think it's just the younger ones now. The older ones can see the steel in the pupil, the sneer in his smile.

And Eddie. Everytime he knows Trev's around, seems like he wants to pull the trees from their roots, rock all the houses, banish the bird-song and smother the blue sky in grey. Eddie can't forgive him. Ever. And Eddie's been angry forever anyway. Tries to come across so smooth and all, but he's burning. Madder than hell about the landfill. He got as many people together as he possibly could, petition and all. I represented them. We fought and fought. It didn't matter. Money. All about money. Might even be chemical waste dumped there sometimes. How to prove it? Impossible. They swear it's clean garbage, but I'm not so sure. Neither is anybody else around here.

'The lumber yards.' Eddie's screaming. 'Why them? Why not us?'

'Money,' I say. 'Money, Eddie. It's been a very rare occasion in this part of the world when banks will lend folks of color any large sums of money, so that we can make as much profit as them. Things are easing a little, but don't write home about it yet.'

'Hell,' he says. 'All we've got are churches, funeral parlors, small stores and barber-shops. Maybe a garage or two. No large businesses. No major cash concerns, like corn farms, factories. No places that make you want to step back and say, 'Look at that man, just look at that.'

How to make Eddie realize that everybody is suffering? Blacks and Indians and most poor folk in general. Not that we ever got a fair deal to begin with. Our land taken from us; no land given to them. Work for free and for paucity. And now? With manufacturing like a glance at yesterday, the whole industrial thing is crumbling. Plus, if the schools are rotten, well … So the Indians, or Native Americans, as we are now called, along with all the other peripheral folk, are still trying to find a way.

Now, we've got the Reservation. And the 'purity.' And our presiding Chief. But I know about the desperation. The fear. The word said to our faces that would silence and obliterate us forever. 'Nigger.' Oh God, call me anything, anything, but please don't call me that! You can see it in the driven, plagued eyes of some of the older folks. Even some younger ones. I remember listening in when Papa told some men from the tribe. He spoke as if he had rehearsed this for an award-winning performance:

They brought Little Bear and Striking Arrow from Oklahoma. Pure Indian. Proven. Set them out amongst the women like a red river running. Then organized our tribe. That was around the beginning of this century. After two hundred years of white waves washing over us and black bait catching us, we were once again crimson and courageous and sure of who we were.

So they wished. They hoped. They waited. Yet great-grandfather had red hair and blue eyes. Little yellow-tops bobbed up and down among the vegetable gardens and black-berry babies sang songs in the streams. But it was better than before. From 1680 onward there were no more Indians to be found in this county's records. We were all Colored people. From 1924 we were all red again. What would we be by tomorrow morning?

At sixteen, I looked in the mirror and saw pretty. Yes, I was. Very pretty. According to anybody's standards, I decided. My long, long burnished black hair, my eyes like almonds and skin like the inside of a Redwood tree. Tall and leggy and lithe. Like a gazelle. I jumped and frolicked and flourished. My recently widowed and wealthy aunt called for me to come and live in the city. Away from home, in a city of comfort and class, I learned new tricks for our age-old problems. Everything was bigger — schools, houses, shops, books and wallets. Only one thing seemed to shrink: the ability of anyone to tell the truth about themselves.

There was a slick sound to the words, a quick glide away from anything that had a depth of inquiry. Appearance was all: a radiant smile and a watchful eye. Manners. Manners and moist lips.

Lips to entice the right man, the upright man. My lips never seemed to stay together too long, though. Mouth open, words jabbing at the air, questions were always on my tongue. I was a nuisance, an upstart. A problem to be dealt with. I decided just to be an inquisitive, noisy, little 'Indian' girl. I lost the stereotype and found myself.

I had made a beginning. A start. People were curious and came not necessarily because they needed legal advice, but just to see a woman sitting in her Tidewater office talking about the law. Especially the men. Couldn't quite grasp the fact that one of their women could carry this through. Justice. That cloudy expression that made their smiles strain to the tips of their ears and cause their teeth to jut forward and you to jump back.

Questions assailed me: 'Why? Where? Is it possible? Doesn't the law say …? And I've decided to …' But usually it was, 'What can I do?'

After years of acquiescence and placation, the fight-spirit stirred again.

'Where are our bones? The left-lives of our ancestors? We want them back. They belong to us.'

Great universities and renowned professionals spent years staring at our mummified marrow, which brought them world-wide recognition, but little understanding. How could they fathom who we were by holding sapless limbs in their hands when they could never hear our voices or look into our eyes?

Black eyes in black-red faces pulled in and pinched. What to do with the knowledge that half their limbs lie in a laboratory and the other half in the labyrinth of a slow, furling river?

I sat in the waiting room and let my eyes spin from frame to frame. On every wall and on clustered surfaces, were photographs of grim, white ancestors with powdered wigs and bristling beards like thickets and large, flinty eyes. Who among them knew my great-grandmother? Intimately? My people were linked and locked to these grey and black replicas. We walked amongst each other, ghosts living and dead, unable to see the sameness, the difference. And when we did, a high laugh and an averted eye were our only acknowledgements.

'Good morning, Miss Bainbridge,' he said.' Sure is good to see you. You looking quite lovely, as usual.'

He was long. And very lean. With his adam's apple protruding so far out that his paisley print bow-tie danced fitfully on his neck. Mr Benjamin Bainbridge. He, one of mine; I, one of his; somewhere along our family's clouded genealogy.

As he crossed his legs in a slow, feminine arc, his voice became thick with a sweet, sickly tone: 'Now, Darlene, why do you and your folks want to stir up such trouble? Y'all are doing real well down here. At least y'all ain't on no dry reservation in the middle of nowhere. All y'all people is just where you always were. Same land as when old Smith came wandering in. What you need some bones for? Sacred burial ground! Now y'all know, y'all ain't got no idea where the hell that is now. Why don't you just let by-gones be by-gones? Besides, these academics might find out stuff about you and your people y'all ain't never known. Now personally, I would think that would be much more exciting than trying to get all them dry bones back. Dry bones. Get it? Remember that Negro song?'

I told him that the tribe would petition and send it to the Federal Government, as many other tribes in America were doing. 'You've had your day, Bainbridge. Now it's ours.'

He laughed, then turned as hard as granite. 'So you're a lawyer now. I remember you with mud on your little dress and your knees and feet all dry and ashy. I remember all your people coming to me for help and guidance. And I gave it. I was, and still am, a fair-minded man. And now, here you come trying to give me a difficult time. Trying to show you're better than me. Well, you've got a little more to learn, Darlene, 'cause it ain't gonna be as easy as you think.'

Then his lips slashed across his face. 'And anyway, you and I know that your bones and my bones most likely got the same color marrow.'

As I started the engine and leaned back into my seat, I wondered if it was all worth it? Would this fight for what was left of ourselves be able to change us? Stop us from running like wild elk towards the American good life? I sped past the school with its new bright-orange bricks, and all the conspicuous chrome on the motorcycles dotting the yards. Pronounced prosperity.

Tidewater tarries no longer. We are fast catching up with all the new wonders of this world-on-speed. But even as I fly along in the fantastic lane, I ask myself, will we soon forget to put our ear to the ground and hear our calling?

Picnic

'Well, we been talkin about doin somethin excitin round here for a month of Sundays and ain't done a damn thing yet. What ya'll think? Should we really try this time? I think this be the best time, with Trevor and Charlotte and all. Yes, let's get together, have us some serious fun and praise the Lord. Come on. Let's have a picnic.'

Half of Tidewater County grunted when they heard the news. I knew that many of these folks could squeeze out a, 'How ya'll doin this mornin', or, 'Sure be a beautiful day,' but sustained conversation was not on the agenda. Strained politeness was the answer to hundreds of years of problems.

With a determination and excitement neither of us could quite fathom, Darlene and I managed to stir the county up.

'Charlotte, get on away from here. I ain't thinkin 'bout no picnic. Why in the world would I want to sit around for hours with a whole buncha peoples I tries to avoid? But girl, seein that look in your eyes is worth it though. Maybe the childrens need to see some gatherin, some kind of comin together. Plus, Trevor down here and I done heard Darlene is 'bout to win that case she and Eddie been workin so hard on. Maybe this here should be a celebration.' Aunt Mary paused, moved the toothpick from one side of her mouth to the other, and then allowed a thin, slow smile to cross her face. 'OK,' she said. 'Count on me.'

Soon, houses buzzed: 'Well, how about some coconut cake? And an upside-down pineapple one. Of course, we gotta have chocolate.'

'No. ya'll. We need to be thinkin about more nourishin stuff: fried chicken, potato salad, collards, succotash, biscuits, macaroni and cheese, ribs and all good things like that.'

'Of course, we know that all that's necessary. We was just tryin to get them frills right.'

As Tidewater bubbled, cars groaned back from supermarkets and baskets burst from countless gardens. The people had an electric charge. It was a day away from hopelessness, anger, emptiness and just plain ennui. This picnic was going to be something to remember.

'Here come Charlotte. You know, she dressed to the nines and it ain't nothin but a picnic. Wearin all that linen stuff. Child, you know it always wrinkled. But it real expensive. She nice and all, but I swear, she still got them northern, siddity ways. Sure is a shame about her Momma, though. Now that was a special lady. Always had a smile and a sweet word for everybody. They say she just sit up in bed now and stare. Don't say nothin to nobody. The Lord sure work in mysterious ways. And that husband of hers, well, ain't nobody miss him, I don't think. Oh, he was good sometimes, but you could always see that mean bit around his lips. Couldn't fool nobody with his "I'm so nice" airs. As quiet as Estelle is, they say he one talking fool. Pretty mixed up, too. I mean, I heard that he sometime get confused about his manhood. Can you imagine? Preston, the man who thought every woman in the world wanted him. Hah!'

'Come on. We supposed to be gettin together, not tearin apart. Put a smile on and let's get to it. Ain't right to be pinchin up your mind against people. We's all family today and girl, what a day it's gonna be.'

I moved away from all the women who were chattering and getting the picnic tables together and watched the approaching car. Sadie came next, trying to coax Franklin out of his seat. 'Come on outta there! What kind of foolishness? Sittin in this hot, ol beat-up car, spittin tobacco out the window. Might as well come outside and mess up the whole place with your nasty ol' juice.'

'Aw, get on away from me, woman.'

Franklin's raspy voice turned heads as he dragged himself out of the car. When Sadie walked away, Franklin pulled a bottle from his overall side pocket. He smiled at it, pushed it back inside and patted his rear overall pocket. Then he looked up and gave, to no one in particular, a wide, pernicious grin.

Franklin was thinking, as he nodded to all the folks there, 'I know what's in they minds. They laughin at me about the different childrens and all. Plus, they remembers that Safe Spot. Can't nobody forget it. Can't nobody speak of it, neither. It just clings to everythin and everybody round here like this ol tar from the road that never come out, no matter what you do to it. They think I'm shame. But I'm not shame. I'm gonna show these peoples. I'm still a man and I'm doin just fine.'

He pressed his feet into the earth so hard that each step seemed an affirmation of his existence. He turned his head from side to side, his eyes flitting all the while; they had a raw neediness in them, on a search for the calming influence: blonde bar-baby, bracelets and all.

The area was beginning to fill up. Steamy, sweet-sour smells overtook the salt of the river. Voices welled up with laughter that lashed the trees and feet flattened the green-brown grass that led down to the bank.

'Ya'll come on over here and get some of these ribs.' Eddie was the first one to the table, getting his pick of the best.

Trevor had rolled up by then, but leaned against his silver Mercedes, looking very buttoned-up and ill at ease, when he heard Eddie say, 'Baby, this here is the best. You got to try this. Lean on over so's I can plant one on you. I'm gonna give you the best sugar you done ever had, honey.'

Trevor heard the four lips, moist and smacking and he looked as if he were going to be sick to his stomach. His head downward, his complexion tinged with green, he walked away from the groaning tables and the crowds.

I was really enjoying everybody and everything. Somehow these folks had come together and the air was singing. Huge barrels of ice with beer dotted the place. Tables filled to overflowing with every kind of taste, color and smell, enticing you to eat beyond your capacity. All of this taking place under a sun-filled sky that wrapped you in warmth, with the tranquil touch of a summer's day.

A few hours passed and the decibel level had jacked up; laughter and loud games everywhere. As I sat on the bench, eating my second helping of fried chicken, Trevor approached. The booze had loosened his gait and the smile and swagger were in place. Just as he started to say, 'Charlotte,' another, more forceful voice cracked through the jubilee. Abrasive and breathless with anger, Franklin was shouting as he swayed back and forth on top of a picnic table:

'Ya'll listen here. Ya'll think I'm some stupid bastard. I ain't no such thing. I been kind to most of you and your kin when I shoulda killed your asses. Ya'll know which ones I'm talkin bout. The oh-so-special ones. You're supposed to be pure-blooded Indians, or Native Americans, or whatever. I'm part of ya'll, but since the red outdid the black, I ain't nothin in ya'll books. Well, I calls you some coward-ass mothafuckas. Mean and uncarin sons-of-a-bitch. When them bastards came lookin for my Papa, ya'll started runnin in every direction until somebody got tired and opened their big, ugly mouths.

'You sure wasn't runnin away from us before, in them ol days, when you be gettin together, makin that love and them black-red babies. Been doin it for so long, be hard to tell where anybody be comin from. Specially with the white folks slippin in all the time, wanted or not.

'But then, somebody got real smart and that purification started, so as to be gettin that red skin back and that black hair straight. So when those pointed-head sheets came, well ya'll put notices on your doors sayin: "We's Indians." How ya'll live in your minds after that, I don't know. But then, I been havin real trouble in my mind 'cause all I wanted to do was to get next to ya'll womens that look almost white. But that still don't erase what done happened here. Why don't we all just go on to the safe-spot. Get the whole thing over with. What ya'll say?'

As Franklin struggled to get himself down from the table, people were frozen and stunned into silence. It was if a huge hand had come and wiped away the warmth in the air and the yellow orb in the sky. Everything and everybody was grey, all the joy drained away.

Franklin's foot missed its target and he fell to the ground. He laughed, venom filling the silent spaces and reached into his pocket. Everyone sucked in the air and held it still until the flask appeared and reached his lips.

'Ya'll seem to be forgettin what done happened. Ya'll want me to remind you? Tell you that Papa forgot he was a black man for about two minutes and lost his life. Just tryin to be a person and they whittled him down to just about nothin. You old ones remember. And the young ones done heard.

'The KKK came ridin through this county as if huntin for wild animals. Them white bitches done told they husbands, they boyfriends, they fathers and they brothers 'bout how this black man with straight hair be takin advantage of they poor little white woman who be so sick. So sick my ass. She be drunk.

'Then them white-ass, white-sheeted bastards come lookin for Papa. Be bangin on every door, threatenin to kill everybody round here, if nobody told them where he was.

'Well, one of you Indians sure did oblige. Ya'll could see, from a long time ago, that this sick, white mothafucka be thinkin you better than any niggers. Could see that you might have a chance to live, at least a little bit better than these poor-assed black folks. So, ya'll just went on and did what any good citizen would do. Help those in need. Pointed your fingers and your tongues straight to our door.

'Them KKK's had a picnic that night, right at the safe-spot. That's where they hunted down my Papa. He knew they was comin after him and he run and run to a place near the river, where there be all that deep thicket. He called it his safe-spot. Figure nobody find him. But they did; they found his ass with them hound dogs and ya'll gibberin mouths.

'They strung him up, swingin, with no more dick, no balls, no ears, eyes poppin. They built them a fire and cooked him, as well as some weiners. Laughed and drank bourbon. Had the wives and children come down for the fun. And all your asses was safe. Ya'll shoulda come down too. Had a look, had a laugh.'

Then Franklin leaned back so far we thought he would fall, but he braced himself and stood upright. Fumbling in his back pocket, he pulled out a gun:

'Now. This be my turn. For Papa, for Papa.'

He started laughing and gurgling and whirling around, with the gun held high in the air. Shots pierced the sky. And, as if following a command, the rains came. People scattered, ran to their cars or skittered down the road. Franklin continued roaring, running towards the river. He reached the bank, sent up a wail, shot his gun for the last time and jumped into the river at the Safe Spot.

The sand filled his mouth along with the salt water and perhaps he believed that this had cleansed his poor, tortured soul. Thinking he had finally passed on to another place, he heard Sadie's voice rip open the silence, 'Get up, you stupid son-of-a-bitch. You in the water, but it ain't but about a foot or two deep here. You happy with yourself now? You done made sure that nobody come near us now. We be alone for certain, you with your big mouth.'

Franklin raised himself to his knees, body dripping, and cried a cry that tore his insides apart. The sound flew out of him and resonated from side to side of that river.

EATING DISORDERS

DOTS of brown, blue, green and grey — all their eyes in a white sea. Why did we have to meet in this place? Nothing but the old guard seated in their chairs as if the Confederacy was still a point of argument. They slid their eyes across my space, lifted their brows and took a simultaneous and audible suck of air.

Northerners could never quite get it: Spanish, Sicilian, Puerto Rican, Costa Rican, Brazilian, Jewish? Anything but! 'No. Not that. Really? Gosh, you could never tell. Well, you sure fooled me.'

These buttoned-down, oxford-cloth, seer-sucker Southerners knew their own, though. A few coughs, shuffle of seats, caustic calls to the old, black waiter and everyone settled in for the duration.

The shirt was sienna with flashes of gold. Stepped in almost before him. But the show was his. No contest. The color a bold compliment to a face both sensual and ruthless. Vulnerable. Vast in possibilities. The variegated garden of America, all in the rise of a cheek-bone, the spark of a smile. Trevor: everybody wanted a piece, nobody the whole.

Stepped straight to the table and let everyone gasp and whisper. The room restless with agitation. Against their better judgement, had to admit it. He was who he was; everybody's dream of nights to remember, but not to be told. And days and days of delirium.

He spoke and there it was. More pronounced than in the movies. That choke in the sound. Sexy. As if he wanted to get close to you so badly, he had to halt himself, stop the emotion. Reconsider.

The breath was warm and sour-sweet, just like the first time by the river.

'Charlotte. Aren't you glad to see me? You look haunted. I know I still got something going for me. Give me a smile at least, girl.'

I flipped my eyes up and took it in. Yes. All there. Always there. It would never go from me totally. Never. Like the grainy, salt-water I seemed to taste in my mouth from time to time. That river water that coated our tongues all tangled in each others' greedy mouths.

He was talking a wild streak. Teeth lighting up the room. I could hear him as if underwater:

'Hope you didn't mind coming here. Wanted to shake up these old farts. Loved to see the look on their faces when this home-boy strode in. Just about stroke-time. These old geezers holding their hearts, 'cause I got America's in the palm of my hand …'

Couldn't hear at all now. I was submerged.

In the water, it was sliding. Slipping in and out of me. The bite of the sun on my neck as I stood up to take him in, slowly, bent and bursting. His gold, brown face rubbing against mine, back and forth, back and forth. Teeth taking my shoulder, hair turning black to chestnut, face sable to snow. Soft hands and slender fingers in my mouth and mine in hers. On sand, open and thirsting. Her juices running in and through me with the river water. She his face. He hers. I took them as one. Color-burst. The heat of happiness piercing. I melted into myself.

'Did you hear what I said? You don't seem to be here at all. Are you all right?'

'Sorry. Felt a little faint. This heat down here makes my mind fly off.'

'Yeah, I know what you mean. Well, maybe we both need to eat. I'm famished. How about you? Lobster? Yes? Yes. Some sweet meat for a sweet lady.' He leaned back and flicked his hand at the waiter, as self-satisfaction seemed to blow him up to twice his size.

I knew he couldn't quite believe that I really wasn't into men anymore. You could see him reconstructing reality to suit the film he was making. He sat back a little in his chair, squinted and smiled a satisfied smile. 'Still wants me. Won't though. Married. Thinks I wouldn't cheat. Hard for her not to desire me, though.'

I could almost imagine what he was thinking. That I still wanted him.

Some truth in it, the memory most likely far more interesting than the real thing. Knew he had heard about the rape at college. Probably blamed my change-up on that. Don't know. Think it was a seed planted, in the beginning. Just looking for the right soil and climate to grow. Heard that some Native American tribes revered homosexuals. Thought they were gifted, holy. Couldn't tell that to the folks down here now. Be run off the face of the earth.

He seemed to be uncomfortable, as if whatever he was thinking was far from pleasant. 'I know why we didn't get together. She was always into borderline stuff. Never in the fold. Always on the edge. Her artwork. Music. Friends. So different from people I knew, with their wordy, garbled take on life. Making a mockery of most things I had. Cars and big, brassy houses filled with all those man-made goodies that I could grasp in an instant. These people only had each other. Nobody else would want to listen to them for more than five minutes. Artists do some weird shit anyway. Too bad though. She was a good piece of ass.'

The plate glowing with pink and orange. Claws clutching air in desperation. A small yellow pool to dip in. He plunged. The white, sleek, morsel dunked and devoured. 'Lord, this is some great lobster. So fresh, so succulent. Go on, dive in. The water's fine.'

I began to eat, ghosts gone for a moment. Sucked on the thin, hard casing, tongue poised for the smooth, pointed end. Digging and prying. Lips buttered and busily making discoveries.

'Have you been listening to the radio lately? Black rap music, I mean. You know, gangsta rap or something. It's disgusting.'

I looked at him and thought, is it worth it? He knows the answer to this question. He just doesn't want to deal. To remember who he is, was, and why our lives get so misconstrued and convoluted in this mad place.

I said, 'It's like the blues. Whitey caught on to a good thing, changed the political to the sexual, kept the stereotype in place and cleaned up. So, what else is new?'

'Well, if everybody is so hip to this, why do these young cats dis their

146

women so?'

'Oh, come on. Money. Because they're powerless. They know the game. No education, no chance. Some of them have been led to believe that a hard dick can beat up anybody and that a gun is your most profound and persuasive tool. Besides, drugs and low self-esteem don't help. Some lead, quite a few follow. Everybody's not a brain-trust, you know. And speaking of following, we were so busy getting out of black neighborhoods that these kids didn't have any middle-class folks to look up to. I sometimes wonder if we shouldn't shoulder a little bit of the blame. Pockets of Tidewater County are headed in the same sad direction, and all anybody is doing is clicking their tongues and shaking their heads.'

His jaw got tight. She always had an answer. Head slightly raised to the right, chin tipped up, pupils drawn in like sharp pencil leads, Charlotte would hold forth. Confident. Cutting. Ever since she was little. His pulse was off-track. He felt stony. Yeah. She was a real pain in the ass.

'Well.' He said it so loudly that people two tables away jumped. "Bout time I got going. Driving up to New York in my new wheels. Need some quality time with myself. Best way I know.'

We both cleared our throats louder than was necessary. He paid the bill and we left.

You couldn't help but relax in this machine. Cool leather, cool air, cool music. Cruising. Grover Washington teasing the tenor and him talking shit. Sounded good. Like those long-ago lost days that I sometimes convinced myself I missed.

A serene scene. Even some young blacks, whites and Native Americans walking together now. Living together. Fighting and crying together. Tidewater County coasting to the new century. Bible-belted, money-mad, calorie-coated and looking for a reason. A reason to accumulate, to bend to the bone for. Breaking backs to buy, they tried not to notice: less money, less medical coverage, less listening, more talk. With laws rescinded and racism on the rampage, it was rush time.

Full speed to the year 2000. Weighted and wealthy they could say, 'I got mine. Yes indeed. Before it was all over, I got mine.'

We drove along watching the heat bend the air, when the pines on the right side of the road seemed to open up. Space straight through to the waterway.

'Trev. Stop here. I'm getting out.'

'What? You crazy? This is nowhere.'

'That's alright. I want nowhere, you understand?'

Trev just couldn't see it: the gravel road that beckoned; the river that reeled in my heart. Yeah, that was the problem. He didn't understand. Never, ever could.

'Sure,' he said, crestfallen. He wanted to smooth things over from lunch, make himself feel better about them somehow. He looked: her face opaque. It was as if a layer had left already.

'Yeah. Sure. So take care of yourself. Come by to see Linda and me sometime. It was great, as always. Just great.'

He kissed a ghost. Lips like dry gauze. Eyes like paperweights.

'See you,' I said, although my vision for the ordinary had completely vanished.

I couldn't leave this place, even when I left. I realised my past was my present and until I and all in this place, accepted that, turmoil would keep hold. As I took off my shoes and approached, the usually yellow-brown, brackish river was clear, enticing. I bent my face to it, brushed its salty surface. Saw all the swirling seasons; the year upon year of yeasty hopes and deracinated dreams. Centuries surging through the currents; restless, looking for peace.

I knew then that I too would swim in this restive parade. I was learning the refrain already; knew each foot-beat, arm-stride. The choruses surged through me, pushing my singular pain into a wider stream, making me take on the temper of Tidewater, from all its yesterdays into all its tomorrows. Making me want to plant some seed of love, some kernel of determination and some embryo of equity; in this place and in all other places where my body rested and my hands touched.

Bright flashes of lemon-light punctured a brooding, violet sky, as I peeled my face from the river. The water rolled down in rivulets, skimmed my lips and was gone. But the salt seeped in and stayed with me — thirsting, from skin to mind to heart.

POCAHONTAS SPEAKS

I sailed on, a token
to peace and patriarchy –
brocaded, stomachered,
emblematic, misconstrued,
I breathed the air
that froze my words forever.

Mouth of the Thames,
shores low and marshy,
felt my soul slip
as I saw my grave
and met my end.

Tidal river take me
toward the spirit-sea
of homecoming,
where I see the future
mirrored in your tortured twin
ever-flowing,
flowing, flowing.

Pocahontas, daughter of Powhatan
Born Mataoka, Werowocomco, c.1595
Died Rebecca Rolfe, Gravesend, 1617

ABOUT SANDI RUSSELL

Sandi Russell is a direct descendant of the Native American tribe that befriended the first English settlers in Virginia, and the African slaves who helped create America. She grew up in Harlem during the Civil Rights era and spent her first thirty years in New York City. Educated at the New York High School of Music and Art, Syracuse University and Hunter College, Sandi taught in the South East Bronx before becoming a professional jazz singer in Manhattan's best venues. Moving to England, she continued to perform with other outstanding musicians, making CDs that include *Incandescent* and *Sweet Thunder*.

In Britain, Sandi Russell developed a parallel career as a journalist and writer, gaining a reputation as an interpreter of American culture. An essay, 'Minor Chords — Major Changes' appeared in *Glancing Fires* (The Women's Press). She co-edited the *Virago Book of Love Poetry* and some of her own poems have been published. Sandi Russell's much-praised book on African American women writers, *Render Me My Song*, appeared on both sides of the Atlantic in 1992. Described as 'women's history that reads like a compelling story', it received a new edition in 2002. Sandi had by then created a powerful show of the same name, performing it throughout Europe and the UK. *ELLA!*, her one-woman show about the life and music of Ella Fitzgerald, also unites Sandi's exceptional gifts as a singer and writer.

Sandi Russell has been publishing short fiction for over a decade. One of her stories appeared in *Daughters of Africa* (Jonathan Cape). *COLOR* is her first novel.

To find out more about the author, go to
www.sandirussell.co.uk

AN INTERVIEW WITH SANDI RUSSELL

This interview took place at the University of Angers, France, where Sandi Russell was guest of honor at a conference on orality in short fiction. It was published in a special issue of the Journal of the Short Story in English, *number 47, Autumn 2006. This edited version is published by kind permission of the journal's editor, Professor Laurent Lepaludier, who conducted the interview with colleagues from the Faculty of Letters.*

Laurent Lepaludier: I would like to introduce Sandi Russell to those who weren't at the concert last night. This time the focus is on Sandi Russell's achievements in fiction, for Sandi Russell is not only a singer, she is also a critic and a writer. Our research centre has been particularly interested in her short-story 'Sister', anthologized in *Daughters of Africa*, which was edited by Margaret Busby.

The oral dimension of Sandi Russell's writing is the reason why we decided to invite her as guest of honor for this conference on orality in short fiction. Her scholarly achievements, her ear for music and sounds, and her writing style, offer a perfect combination for a topic such as ours. So it is a great pleasure for us to be in Sandi Russell's company.

Traditionally – and it is a tradition established more than twenty years ago in this research center – we invite short story writers to read from their works, and answer questions from us and from the floor.

We are grateful that Sandi Russell has accepted this invitation, following such other writers such as Mavis Gallant, Graham Greene, V.S. Pritchett, Muriel Spark, Antonia Byatt, Amit Chaudhuri, Romesh Gunesekera, Olive Senior, Louis de Bernières, John McGahern, Grace Paley and Tobias Woolf. (The interviews are available in a special issue of our *Journal of the Short Story in English*, number 41, Autumn 2003.)

Sandi Russell: I would like to thank Laurent Lepaludier and the entire committee for choosing me for this very special honor. The short story 'Sister' is really the kernel of my current work-in-progress, *Color*. This novel is a multi-voiced narrative about race and sexuality in the twentieth century. Through a range of characters, it also explores Native American/African American exchange.

I originally called the novel *Tidewater*, because it takes place in an area of Virginia where the Atlantic Ocean meets the fresh waters that flow into Chesapeake Bay. Jamestown was the first permanent English colony in North America, where

Powhatan's daughter, Pocahontas, married John Rolfe in 1614, and the first slaves from Africa landed in 1619.

The narrative follows Charlotte, a New York artist, in her quest for her roots in Virginia. As she encounters her relatives across three generations, truths about the place and its history, including 200 years of slavery, and the near obliteration of the original inhabitants, come to light.

Among these relatives are her 'country cousins': Sister (known here as Cousin Sister) and *her* sister, Henrietta. She is supposedly insane, but she is also the linchpin of the novel. I'd like to read for you from the first part of the novel, when Henrietta takes up the story.

....

Audience: Thank you, Sandi, for your reading. It was very powerful, especially the voice of Henrietta. We've been talking, at this conference, about 'other' voices, 'different' voices. When you were reading, it was like you were singing last night – it was like another voice that just came out of you, so beautifully and powerfully. Where does that come from?

Sandi Russell: I don't know where Henrietta came from. It obviously is a part of me somewhere. But I was shocked when this voice came, such a strong voice. Writing is a very strange thing. You can sit down and think you're going to write in a certain way. Half an hour later, you look at this page and it's not anything like you thought it was going to be at all. I think Henrietta is, in a way, a silenced Southern voice that isn't heard very much anymore. That is the best I can do.

Audience: I'm just interested in how writers talk about getting the voice. Margaret Lawrence, a Canadian writer, said that she had to get the voice of Hagar, in *The Stone Angel*, and then it just took her where it was meant to go. As you say, it is a kind of possession.

Sandi Russell: Out of all the characters in *Color*, Henrietta is definitely almost a possession. Through her crazed vision, we learn of the family history, and the history of her people. She even names the ships of the first English settlers in Virginia. So she tells the history of Tidewater in a completely fresh way, because she is mad. But her vision is very clear and very real.

Michelle Ryan Sautour: I'm always very curious about what pushes a person to write, and we've been given some insight into your talent as a writer. Can you tell us what brought you to write fiction?

Sandi Russell: I think music had a lot to do with it. I've been singing off and on since the age of four, and singing is a form of story-telling. So, when I wasn't literally making musical sounds, I still had some kind of impetus to tell stories. I was also a voracious reader, so it just seemed the other thing that I could do was a way of continuing to make music, because I try to write in a musical way.

Laurent Lepaludier: An old-time song is quoted in 'Sister', 'Come on Baby, Come on Back Home', as well as the hymn, 'Precious Lord, Take my Hand'. Can you tell us about the type of music they are and what they suggest to you?

Sandi Russell: The first one is a sort of blues tune that 'yours truly' made up. And the blues is where jazz comes from. I think the blues is always very evocative of African American culture, so maybe that's why I use the blues. 'Precious Lord, Take my Hand' is a gospel hymn that I love. I just used it because it's one of my favorite songs.

Michelle Ryan Sautour: According to your book, *Render Me My Song*, this use of music is a trend in African American writing. You've talked about how Margaret Walker used poetic forms based on jazz and blues rhythms and how Gwendolyn Brooks uses the ballad and the Negro spiritual. Could you say a bit more about this?

Sandi Russell: Music is very important to black Americans for many reasons. Not only because it is a lovely, relaxing thing, but because it holds a great deal of political significance and significance for our historical survival. In slavery days, secular chants and spiritual songs were used, not only to help ease the burden of the difficult work that slaves had to do, but also to send coded messages to each other to enable them to escape on what was called the 'Underground Railroad'. So, music has always been an integral part of African American existence. It has been a means of relief, release, joy and, as I said before, survival.

Laurent Lepaludier: In your works, orality can obviously be heard in the dialogues, especially in *Tidewater* – I mean, *Color* – and, obviously too, the narrative has an oral quality. When you write, do you actually voice the narrative out loud, or is it a mental voice?

Sandi Russell: Sometimes, when I write, I do read out loud to make sure the rhythm is flowing in the manner that I want and it's giving the feeling I want to evoke. But it's usually all in my head.

Michelle Ryan Sautour: Something that has come up a lot during the conference is the question of speech patterns and identity, the idea of using speech as a sort of mask. You are adopting an identity, you are using speech as a sort of mask. What are your thoughts on that subject?

Sandi Russell: Do you mean how do I arrive at these different personae? In black speech, there are many gradations of persona. A great deal of African American speech is used to mask what is really being said. I'm thinking of Zora Neale Hurston quoting, 'Got one face for the world to see, 'nother for what I know is me. He don't know, he don't know my mind.' Is that what you are talking about?

Michelle Ryan Sautour: No, but it's a very interesting answer. [Laughter.]

Audience: Charlotte's male cousin, Eddie, goes fishing and while he's taking himself off to the river, he gives a whole thing on the ecology of the place. That is a very different speech from Henrietta's, isn't it?

Sandi Russell: *Color* is what Henry Louis Gates calls a very speakerly text. I use monologues where characters like Eddie and Henrietta speak directly to the reader. They define themselves through the way they speak, the words they use. At least, I try to define who they are through the way they speak. Not necessarily all that they say, but through their speech patterns as well.

Michelle Ryan Sautour: You are a writer, and you are also a literary critic. What led you to write your book *Render Me My Song: African American Women Writers from Slavery to the Present*?

Sandi Russell: I realized, living in Great Britain, that very few people knew about any African American writers at all. I felt that it was necessary to let them know about all the great black women writers that had published. It was a very exciting time in America because a lot of nineteenth-century writers who had not been heard of were literally being unearthed. Henry Louis Gates Jr's work in bringing them to light was an impetus for writing the book. I also felt that a lot of ideas were being tossed around by academics that the regular reader, the interested reader of African American literature, should know about. So I set myself the task of trying to make these ideas, which you discuss in such a complex way, just a bit clearer for regular readers. I think it was all of those things together that inspired me to write the book.

Michelle Ryan Sautour: Could you comment on the title you chose? The meaning of *Render Me My Song*?

Sandi Russell: It just means, 'give me my due', 'give what is owed to me'. That is essentially what it means.

Michelle Ryan Sautour: We've talked, during the conference, about the pressures of the publishing industry. Could you talk about how this has limited certain ways of writing?

Sandi Russell: The 'white establishment' still has major power in publishing in the Western world. But there are smaller publishing houses that are African American based, black British and Caribbean based, and so there are voices heard that might not have been heard at all if it weren't for them.

It's difficult for any artist, be they black or white, to get into a reputable publishing house. And, if you do get in, there are often restrictions: certain stereotypes are still expected from black writers. Plus, they want a very clear-cut narrative. So it's not just a problem of coming from a particular ethnic group, but also the way we are told to write in order to make a bestseller.

Ben Lebdai: 'Not to know is bad. Not to ask is worse.' You quote this African proverb at the start of your book *Render Me My Song*. It suggests that people are themselves responsible if they are ignorant of things, rather than external influences.

Sandi Russell: I didn't mean it as literally as that. I just meant that curiosity is a good thing. Essentially, I was saying 'You should go beyond your own little sphere if you can – you could learn something new and exciting.'

Ben Lebdai: You have written that when you were young, you felt cheated, because black writers, both men and women, were ignored. You used almost the same words as Ngugi wa Thiong'o, when he recalled his education in colonial Kenya – the English literature courses when African writers were not on the program, and when the African environment was ignored in favor of daffodils and cottages.

Sandi Russell: I went to school in the center of Harlem and most of my teachers were black. But they were not allowed, at that time, to teach African American literature. We did have one week though, when there was a lot of talk about Langston Hughes and Paul Lawrence Dunbar and George Washington Carver and the peanut. [Laughter.] That was about it. So I would say that, when I was going to school, I learned very little about black American writing, or even black American culture for that matter.

Ben Lebdai: As a former teacher, what role do you think orality might play in today's education, especially in certain schools or parts of New York, say?

Sandi Russell: I think speech is highly valued now, in fact, there is more talking than reading in modern media. Also, in African communities as well as African American communities, the oral tradition is very strong. I think that would be a means of getting through to students. It ties in with their culture, and that's essential.

Ben Lebdai: For the first time, in an Angers conference, we have a writer, a critic, and a singer in one person. Can you tell us what are the benefits of combining these genres?

Sandi Russell: Somebody said to me 'What's it like to be a singer and a writer?', and

I said, 'The singing is an extroverted kind of exercise. The writing is introverted, you're very much inside yourself.' It's hard sometimes to do both, but at the same time, each informs the other.

Audience: Have you ever written a song?

Sandi Russell: Until recently, I hadn't. But I've written poems, and the lyrics of two songs that have been set to music for my forthcoming CD, *Sweet Thunder*. And of course as a jazz singer, I'm always improvising.

ACKNOWLEDGEMENTS

I am grateful to so many who have helped to bring this work to fruition, among them: Maya Angelou, Louise Gibbs, Olivia James, Lynn Kilgore-Hendy, Dolly McPherson, Hugh and Lotte Shankland and Susan Walker.

In researching this book, I have drawn on recent scholarship in African American, Native American and American history. The poems 'The River Speaks' and 'Pocahontas Speaks' first appeared in the *Morden Poets* anthology.

Especial thanks go to Judith Mashiter of Mosaic, for her patience and expertise, to Claude Paquette for her striking artwork, to Anne Stevenson and Peter Lucas for their support and encouragement, and to Diana Collecott, for her editorial assistance and enduring belief in my work.